A Courtship at Linlithgow

Thistle and Rose
Book 1

Kate Robbins

ARE YOU SIGNED UP FOR DRAGONBLADE'S BLOG?

You'll get the latest news and information on exclusive giveaways, exclusive excerpts, coming releases, sales, free books, cover reveals and more.

Check out our complete list of authors, too!

No spam, no junk. That's a promise!

Sign Up Here

www.dragonbladepublishing.com

Dearest Reader;

Thank you for your support of a small press. At Dragonblade Publishing, we strive to bring you the highest quality Historical Romance from some of the best authors in the business. Without your support, there is no 'us', so we sincerely hope you adore these stories and find some new favorite authors along the way.

Happy Reading!

CEO, Dragonblade Publishing

"…And, since thou art a king, be thou discreet,
Herb without virtue hold thou not of such price
As herb of virtue and of odour sweet;
And let no nettle vile, and full of vice,
Mate him to the goodly fleur-de-lis,
Nor let no wild weed full of churlishness
Compare her to the lily's nobleness.

Nor hold thou no other flower in such dainty
As the fresh Rose, of colour red and white;
For if thou dost, hurt is thine honesty
Considering that no flower is so perfect,
So full of virtue, pleasance and delight,
So full of blissful angelic beauty,
Imperial birth, honour and dignity…"

The Thistle and the Rose, by William Dunbar

CHAPTER ONE

Linlithgow, Scotland, 1504

A TOURNEY WAS always considered an exciting and joyous occasion. Ladies and lords donned in their very best attire, the castle grounds overflowing with the finest flowers, exotic animals, and culinary delights. So why did Marion's belly flutter with anxiety on this bright sunny morn? The reason was simple. She was to be presented this day to the king and queen as an eligible maiden who may attend the king's court.

The whole arrangement was ridiculous by her estimation. She could very well find herself a suitable match all on her own without the mortification of being paraded and gawked at by sweaty old men who wanted a filly with which to breed.

Her only comfort was the relationship between the king and queen. Of she, this young enigma of only fifteen summers, it was widely rumored they had not officially consummated the marriage which had occurred last year. At the request of her family, her husband would not breed with her until she reached a more appropriate age of at least sixteen. He being twice her age, this was more than a reasonable demand.

Marion herself was seventeen summers and did not feel at all ready to enter the marriage state—her parents, of course, had quite a different opinion on the subject, her mother in particular.

"Are you so enamored with your visage, that you will stare at yourself forever?" her younger sister Alice asked.

Marion jumped a little at the sound of her voice, forgetting that she had not closed the door completely after returning to her chamber from breaking her fast.

"I am merely wondering why I must wear all these layers in this heat."

"Oh, sister, you look beautiful as always, and I am sure the castle will provide an appropriate amount of shade. I am also certain the lords and knights will keep you distracted from your irritation with your gown," she said as she picked at Marion's skirts.

Her mother had the crimson brocade brought from England as a gesture to impress the queen. With a square neckline, and long floor-length sleeves, her gown was edged with thick gold leaf-shaped embroidery dotted with thistles. A perfect marriage to showcase her Scottish heritage with the English fabric. Her mother should have been a politician. While the gown was lovely and certainly accentuated her curvaceous figure, Marion would prefer watching from the sidelines versus thrust into the center of the court's attention.

"Will you wear the gable hood mother had fashioned for you?" Alice asked.

"Absolutely not," she said. "I will wear my hair uncovered with a small floral wreath as I would if we were entertaining guests here. Mother will not present me as entirely English."

"Daughter will do as she is told," her mother said from the doorway.

Marion turned to view the look of determination on her mother's face, but relaxed when she spied her father closely behind. His presence always gave her courage.

"I will present myself to their majesties as a Scottish maiden, not an English one. I have agreed to this uncommonly heavy and restrictive gown, but that is all the concession I will make," she said and folded her arms across her chest, tilting her chin ever so slightly up in the air. Childish maybe, but the point needed to be made.

"You look like a princess, yourself," her father said and made his way to her to kiss her forehead.

Her mother would know better than to challenge when her father had taken her side. She had often called them two peas in a pod and claimed they conspired against her. The suggestion wasn't entirely untrue, but it wasn't pleasant to have it voiced in such a way and so often.

"I merely want her to be accepted and noticed on this of all days."

"Och. Anyone who does not see the radiant beauty that is my daughter, is not worthy of our notice, dear wife. Now let us make haste; the king has offered us seats under his canopy for the tourney opening, and I for one will appreciate the shade."

Alice quickly placed a wreath of hawthorne blossoms onto Marion's hair and kissed her cheek. "I look forward to hearing every last detail about the lords, and I mean every detail."

There was no doubt in Marion's mind that when it was time for Alice's presentation at court, she would embrace every last second of it and thrive in the attention. If only they could trade places for the day.

"Come, lass, make haste." Her mother shooed her out of her chamber and down the stairs to the front of the manor they kept while in Linlithgow. Their larger estate was farther south of Edinburgh, but her mother insisted this summer, they would reside in Linlithgow so as to be closer to the king and his young queen.

The ride to the palace was not overly long; however, being crammed into the small carriage they had secured with her fussing mother and eye rolling father could truly be considered torture straight from the dark ages.

"Mother, my gown is low enough."

"There is nothing wrong with drawing attention to your assets."

"There is also nothing wrong with leaving a little to the imagination. No daughter of mine will appear like she just stepped out of a common brothel," her father said.

And on it went until they finally reached the palace entrance. Marion had only ever heard stories of the delights inside the palace walls. Now she was about to see for herself, and her excitement was enough to momentarily quell the fluttering in her belly.

The carriage stopped and a footman flicked back the canvas, then placed a step at the rear. Her father stepped out, followed by her mother, and she last. She accepted the footman's hand and noted how his gaze flickered across her neckline then, realizing he'd been caught gawking, quickly masked his bold act.

As soon as she was past him and sheltered by her parents walking ahead through the courtyard, she shifted her bodice slightly up to allow for a little more coverage. It took a great deal of her courage to walk forward rather than retreat to the carriage and insist she be returned to the manor.

A loud screech drew her attention upward. A hawk circled above then dived sharply downward toward that which it had hunted. The distraction was just enough to steady her. The moment she entered the inner courtyard, all other thought vanished. Painted men walked on long sticks and blew fire in bright orange streams, another pretended to push against something invisible. Marion stared harder to see what could possibly hold him back. But there was nothing. The sight was mesmerizing.

"Keep up, lass," her father said ahead of her.

The aroma of roasting meat was enough to tantalize the senses until she spied a table topped with all sorts of pastries and pies. Other tables were topped with every sort of trinket imaginable, and more colored fabric than any she had ever seen hung from wooden dowels. Marion wanted to explore each and every item and taste each delight, but her father still ushered her forward.

Through another doorway, they went to the back of the palace where a long seating area was built and covered with a canopy to provide much needed shade. A light breeze which blew in across the small loch just on the other side of the tourney area was a comfort, but would not be enough respite from the hot sun.

She followed her parents to the stairs leading to their seats, and true to his word, the king had reserved three seats just behind and to the right of his own. Other guests had arrived, and for the first time since she'd donned the gown, Marion was less conscious considering the degree of over-the-top ornate headdresses worn by most of the other ladies present. Some wore the very old-fashioned butterfly hennin, while others opted for her mother's new preference in the gable hood. Marion preferred her own floral wreath with her hair uncovered to any of those. As a single maiden, she did have a choice; once she married, she would be expected to cover her hair. Yet another reason to delay the act. Still, it was clear who amongst them wanted to appear as the most elite based on the lavishness of their appearance. Truth be told, they likely fit in more than she at this point.

As they were about to take their seats, the king and queen made their entrance and so everyone remained standing until offered the appropriate acknowledgement. The king turned and nodded at her father then flicked his gaze to her. His features were pleasing, and he held a kind countenance as he smiled.

"My gratitude for joining us this day," the king said to Marion's father. "'Tis a fine one for a tourney."

"Aye, Your Majesty. 'Tis that indeed," her father said.

In truth, her father had confessed to her he was in hopes of securing a position with the king. He'd been acting as Lord of Parliament, but that wasn't official. This invitation may apparently secure that. Marion understood her part in the game. For that was all this was—she was a token to be gambled for a larger prize. The thought of it made her sick to her stomach.

She noted the queen had not turned to acknowledge them and wondered about this young woman and her thoughts on being in an even worse state than Marion who was at least of marrying age.

Long silver horns sang their happy notes to gather everyone's attention. The king stood and raised his arms wide, turning to the left then right. Marion could see the man's smile as he turned their way. It had been widely rumored these tourneys were the most joy in which the king engaged. Looking around at the spectacle that was the palace grounds, she could believe it. For there was certainly no item without full attention. Banners flew depicting the various great families of the land, and even the chairs on which they sat had been decorated with a thistle and rose intertwined, the definitive symbol of the royal's union.

"Welcome. Welcome to our summer tournament. We have much to celebrate! Let the games begin!"

The crowd erupted and Marion could not help but become caught up in the excitement as a dozen men all decked in their polished black, silver, or gold armor rode out before the crowd. They were quite the sight to behold as they rode proud, stopping before their king, visors up and eyes forward. She took in all of their presentation, noting how sturdy they sat atop their horses. Some had been decorated with a ribbon braided into the mane while others had been brushed to a fault, not a hair out of place. As her gaze traveled along the line of entrants, she stopped at the blackest, shiniest armor she had ever seen. The outline of a wild boar was hammered onto the breastplate. She didn't know to which clan he belonged, but was certain the armor had cost a great deal of coin. There was no doubt he was someone of import.

Marion took in the rest of the man then, noticing the broad shoulders, and continued looking up until her gaze locked with striking eyes. His brows pinched as if he sorted some great puzzle. The fluttering she had in her belly earlier was back with a vengeance. The longer they held one another's gaze, the more lightheaded she became. It was as though he saw into her very soul, able to see her discomfort.

Somewhere in the distance a man called out the names of the

entrants, but she was too distracted to pay attention. A heartbeat later, he turned his attention toward the king and with sword in hand, placed it to his heart and bowed his head briefly.

Marion prayed no one had noticed the exchange, least of all her mother who would have them in the marriage bed before the afternoon meal was served. She smiled to herself at the thought as she cast her eyes downward to stare at her traitorous hands that would not stop shaking.

When she found the courage to look up again, the riders had disbursed, all but one who caught her gaze again before riding off to take his place among the other contestants of this, the first element of the games. There would be tests of skills including capturing rings while riding at top speeds, but it appeared the king wanted to kick this tourney off with the highest drama.

A joust.

She somehow had been pierced. Did she really need the visual representation to drive the point home?

The first riders took their places opposite one another and positioned their spears. The black rider was nowhere to be seen.

Hoofs pounded the earth, flicking dirt high into the air as the riders approached one another at top speed. Time seemed to slow as the distance between them closed, and Marion could not help but place her hands to her mouth and hold her breath.

A loud crack broke the moment as the rider approaching from the right directed his spear at the chest of his opponent and upon contact, unseated him instantly. He flew into the air and landed with a thud, his groans erupting from him as soon as he slammed onto the dirt.

Servants ran to him, gathered his horse, and helped him to his feet. The victor returned to the scene and held out his hand as a mark of honor in the interest and spirit of the games. The defeated accepted and the crowd went mad with approval.

Marion sat back in her chair, only just realizing she'd been sitting on the edge. The victor came around to present himself before the king who stood and clapped. The queen then moved for the first time and approached the rider. She took a scarf from her skirts and tied it around the rider's arm. Marion was intrigued. There was much about this event and these practices she would need to learn. Did this mean she could show favor to a preferred rider as well? And why did her mother not tell her to bring extra scarves?

ALEXANDER CAMPBELL SLID off his horse and handed the reins to his steward, Alain.

"Christ, I despise being presented like that. I am certain the king enjoys my discomfort."

"I am certain the king is acting in the interest of the spectators, m'lord," Alain said with a smirk.

Though there was station and wealth between them, in another age, Alexander would consider them equals as men. But they did not live in another age, and propriety demanded Alain not be seen to take liberties with his employer.

In a low voice so that only Alain could hear, Alexander said, "I will expect you to hold your tongue in mixed company, Alain. Not everyone here is as progressive as we."

"My apologies, m'lord. I shall reserve my opinions for another time when they are appreciated and requested."

Alexander was well aware the statement dripped with sarcasm and thankfully was not followed by the usual mock bow.

As if to break the tension, Alain asked, "Do you know why the king moved the tourney straight into the joust?"

"I confess I know not. There has been no mention of skills testing, unless he has something else in mind. He's held so many of these now, perhaps he feels the skills tests are too predictable and boring for the crowd."

Alexander preferred the skills tests to the joust. Too much could go wrong at the hands of an unskilled rider, and plenty had been maimed for the sake of entertainment. But it was the other games played at these events that sickened him. The young flaming haired lass had not even tried to hide her greed as she singled him out with her eyes and then drank him in like she was already counting the new gowns she would purchase to impress him. Och, but it boiled his blood when parents paraded these young lasses around. The two sitting with her had certainly left little to the imagination of their scheming as well.

The sooner he could return to Loch Fyne, the better. Three days of this. It would be a trying time, but he had been especially requested this time and there was no way to avoid King James when he set his mind to something.

"You're up next, m'lord," Alain said.

"Already? Is there no skill in this lot?"

"Aye, besides you, I think not. Maybe we will be sharing a tankard of ale sooner rather than later."

A welcome thought, that.

Alexander mounted his horse and accepted his armor from Alain then waited as his spear was strapped to his arm and the leather belt pulled taut. He drew a deep breath and sized up his opponent who struggled to maintain his balance as his armor was secured to his legs and chest. Most of the time, Alexander was aware of his opponents and of their skills, but this man was a stranger to him. A young man for whom his father had aspirations. Maybe. In any case, there would be little contest, and Alexander could move on to the next match. If this was the only exercise he would get on this trip, he may as well make the best of it.

The riders moved into position, both with the long fence to their right. When the flag dropped, Alexander kicked his heels hard just as a flash of flaming hair came into his view in the stands. He focused hard on his task, lest he be bested, but the hair distracted him just enough that he could not unseat his opponent and so would require another pass.

Again, he moved into position and this time focused only on

the chest of the man before him. He rode hard and closed the distance fast enough to spook his opponent's horse, unseating the man and earning Alexander a point without having to touch him.

Alexander bowed to the defeated man on the ground who looked utterly bewildered and then urged his horse to move until they stood before the king who clapped and smiled broadly. No one came to place a scarf on his gauntlet, but the owner of the flaming hair now had cheeks to match.

CHAPTER TWO

KNOTS COILED IN her stomach as she watched the black rider retreat to the contestant's area. Marion sensed great power in him and somewhere among that a formidable determination telling her this was a man not to be crossed. Her earlier fascination turned to wariness.

"Are you enjoying the games, Lady Marion?" a voice asked, startling her from her musings.

She looked up to find the king addressing her directly. For a moment she mouthed soundless words until her mother nudged her with her elbow.

"Speak, child," she said in a low voice through clenched teeth.

"Aye, Your Majesty. I am very much enjoying the games. My family and I are grateful for the invitation."

"Aye, that we are," her father said. "Quite grateful to Your Majesties for such an honor."

The king's gaze flickered from one of them to the other then landed on Marion again. "Come. You will sit up here with my wife and keep her company. You there," he said to a servant standing to the side, "bring the lady a chair."

Marion didn't know what to make of such a gesture. It was one thing to be invited to share the king's canopy, but quite another to be instructed to keep the queen company.

"It would be my honor, Your Majesty," she said as she walked around to the front row and took the seat beside the queen, offering a shy smile.

The queen herself appeared a timid sort, and who could blame her with her current situation? Marion knew well enough to not speak to royalty unless they initiated the conversation and so she waited what felt like an age before the young woman spoke.

"Do you reside in this area, Lady Marion?"

"Aye, Your Majesty, my family and I have taken a small manor in the town for the summer. Our primary residence is south of Edinburgh."

"I am glad to hear it and will be grateful for the company," she said and glanced to her left. "I find that most of those here do not share my interests."

"May I ask what are your interests, Your Majesty?"

"First of all, if we are to be friends, you and I, you cannot end every sentence with 'Your Majesty.' When it is just us talking as we are now, you may address me as my lady."

Marion smiled. She knew very little about this English queen, but somehow, she already liked her. With only two years between them in age, they would certainly have more in common than she with her husband, though Marion would never speak those words out loud.

"And secondly, I wish you to speak freely with me. No one here does. At home, I had my ladies with whom I could converse. Here I have no one."

"You have someone now, my lady. I am grateful for the company for all I hear is how quickly I am to be married off and of my younger sister's interest in being invited to social events such as these."

"I am envious that you were part of the conversation of your impending nuptials. I was not so fortunate," she said in a low voice so only Marion could hear.

Marion searched the queen's expression. Sadness hid behind her pale blue eyes.

"I am sure you will find happiness, my lady."

As if the words pulled the queen from a distant thought, she shook her head and smiled. "I am very blessed in this life and grateful for all I have. And right now, that includes a new friend for whom I have completely forgotten my manners." She turned to the same servant who had acquired Marion's chair. "Do fetch us some libation."

Moments later, goblets of a golden liquid were handed to the queen and Marion; the king waved away the offering. Marion sipped and refrained from gulping the sweet mead as soon as she tasted the delightful drink. While her family regularly included ale and mead in their meals, none she'd ever had was quite like this.

"Do you like it?" the queen asked.

"Aye, my lady, very much so. 'Tis not like any I've had."

"I have had it made special. They brew it for less time and so it is still sweet, but not as potent."

"'Tis delightful."

"So, tell me, Lady Marion," the queen said with a grin, "have any of the contestants caught your eye? If you were to be married off today and had a say, with whom would you prefer?"

Marion swallowed hard. She had not expected such a bold question. In fact, there was someone who'd drawn her notice, but she was not about to share that with anyone.

"Not yet, my lady."

The queen's eyes narrowed. "Very well, keep your secret if you wish," she said with a smile. "But I will suss it out."

Marion offered a smile in return and a promise to herself she would not allow her gaze to fall too long on any one person, though she was keenly aware at all times where the black rider was positioned.

The jousting matches concluded not long after, thankfully, and the queen suggested they enjoy a small repast in the great hall and then a tour of the menagerie.

The great hall at Linlithgow Palace was longer than it was wide, and Marion was certain could contain a thousand people.

At the head of the hall was a long table on a raised platform decorated with dozens of white roses accentuated with many natural wildflowers and thistles, creating an almost ethereal homage to the joining of the Scottish king and English queen. Everywhere Marion looked, there was some reference to the union.

The queen took her hand and urged her forward. "Come, Lady Marion, you will sit beside me."

Marion had no choice but to follow, though she was a little uncomfortable being seated in front of everyone. Thankfully, her parents followed and took their seats at the top of the first of two long benches that sat perpendicular to the king's table. She looked around as much as she could in a polite way so as not to appear like a gawking schoolgirl. Once the king and queen took their seats, the crowd quickly followed and servants came from what seemed like the stone walls themselves with platters of roasted boar, meat pies, tall cakes in the shape of various birds Marion had never seen before, along with breads and cheeses and so many kinds of fruit. There was likely enough food to feed all of Scotland and the queen had referenced this as a small repast. Marion could not imagine what the evening meal would look like.

"Please enjoy your meal, Lady Marion. It will be many hours before the evening feast."

Marion didn't need to be told twice. As soon as the king filled the queen's trencher with his selected cuts of the roasted boar, Marion chose hers and selected a little of as much as she could reach around her. 'Twas more than she would normally eat, but she was curious to try the food and everyone around her had done the same. Her mouth watered from the first taste of the boar to the delicious cheese and of course a goblet of the never-ending flow of amber mead. She'd never been permitted more than one goblet, but if the queen was truthful in it not being potent, she allowed she could imbibe just a little on this occasion.

Her parents appeared to have their attention focused on her

as much as politely possible while in the company of other lords and ladies with whom they were expected to converse. Between bites of food and answering the queen's questions about Marion's family, particularly her sisters, Marion glanced around the hall from time to time, but found no trace of the black rider. She also acknowledged to herself that he could be wearing anything underneath the black armor and so he could be sitting right in front of her, and she would not know him. Somehow, though, she convinced herself she would know him anywhere.

As soon as the thought struck, her belly fluttered. She glanced again at those sitting at the front of the tables. Her breath released when she spied only those who resembled her own parents, all thick around the middle with graying hair. No black riders there.

"Are you looking for someone?" the queen asked with a grin that was beyond her young years.

"Nay, my lady, I was merely ensuring my parents fared well."

"What are you asking, Lady Marion?" the king asked his wife.

It appeared both of them enjoyed this sort of game. She prayed the queen would not allow him to engage with her on this subject as well, lest she truly have no hope of leaving Linlithgow this evening unencumbered with a betrothal.

"I am asking if she is enjoying her repast, Your Majesty," she said and squeezed Marion's arm in a way the king could not see.

She understood Marion's plight all too well and the potential results that could come from a few choice words of a king.

"Thank you, my lady," Marion said.

As if realizing what she'd done by singling out Marion at the head table, the queen then glanced around the hall and leaned in to speak quietly with her husband. She then turned back to Marion wearing a huge grin.

"Would you like to see my pets?"

"Aye, I would like that very much, my lady."

"The king has excused us from the hall to do whatever we wish for the rest of the afternoon and asks if you've brought a costume for this evening's masque."

Her heart dropped. She was not aware of a costumed event, and she was very sure her mother was not, lest she'd have had her decked out from head to toe in the most ridiculous outfit.

"I confess, I was not aware."

"Oh dear, it must have slipped the king's mind. No matter. We will ensure you and your family are properly decked out and now before we worry about any of that, let us go see the beautiful creatures my husband continues to gift me."

The king rose and then everyone else in the hall did as well. The queen and Marion left the table and informed her parents of their intentions for the afternoon before leaving the hall. The queen assured Marion's mother a costume would be provided for all of them and to not worry about her daughter.

Once out of sight of the members of the hall, the queen hoisted her skirts to Marion's shock and sprinted across the side of the palace and on toward a large, covered structure closer toward the loch, giggling as she went. Marion had to break into a fast pace to keep her in sight at all, never mind catching up with her. By the time she reached the structure, she was winded.

The sounds and sights that caught her eyes then pushed all thoughts of a masque and a black rider from her thoughts. Caught in the stare of a thickly maned lion who roared so loud her chest felt the vibration, Marion was transfixed by his beauty and majesty.

"Come and meet my pets," the queen demanded with a beaming smile.

The woman appeared more like the girl she was in these moments, and Marion's resolve to remain unmarried to an old man solidified. She didn't care what the family connection or gain, she would not be caught in a situation like her new friend, even if the king was a kind man who enjoyed pampering his wife.

ALEXANDER WATCHED TWO young women from his position near the stables that allowed the horses respite from the heat and exercise. He did not have to guess or suppose for a moment who they were. While he did not know the name of the red-haired lass, he did recognize the queen. Maybe the crowd inside was dispersing and so it would be a good time for him to quietly find a goblet of ale and something to keep him going for the rest of the day.

The air was considerably cooler inside the palace versus outside. Though the air off the loch offered a slight comfort, 'twas much more comfortable inside.

Alexander found a quiet corner to sit and enjoy some of the sumptuous feast in peace, but not for long.

"There you are," Alain said. "Everyone has been asking for you."

"And that is precisely why I have been attempting to enjoy my repast in peace. With no help from you for drawing attention to me."

He didn't really mean to criticize his friend, but he'd hoped for a few more moments of quiet.

"Ahhh, you mean you are not excited to meet Lady Fraser and her daughter, Lady Cora?"

"You know I am not."

"And what about Lady Gordon and her daughter Lady Marjorie?"

"Not interested in meeting them either."

"Well, they are interested in meeting you, so you had better finish your food, clean the meat out of your teeth, and do your duty to your king and mingle with his guests. It appears his wife and a new friend have removed themselves from the hall, so he is being accosted by every hungry mother in the palace right now looking for you."

Great. That's exactly what he wanted to avoid and knowing his king as well as he did, the man's patience for Alexander's absence would not last long. King James thrived on his guests intermingling, and if you were invited to a gathering of his, you were expected to be present to be entertained, but also entertain in return.

Sighing, he wiped his mouth and scraped his tongue across his teeth then bared them for Alain in a mock grimace.

"Aye, they look clean," he said with a grin. "Now go and flatter the fillies."

It was a cruel way to think of these young ladies. He was sure they had plenty of fine attributes among them; however, he despised the manner in which they were paraded in front of eligible men. Too many times he'd seen a mother tug on a lass's neckline or worse, push her so that she would bump into him. Nay, this was not what he would consider an enjoyable gathering.

"There you are, Argyll," the king said. "We have been looking all over for you. Where had you gotten yourself off to?"

"I do apologize, Your Majesty. I was securing my horse. He was restless and needed some extra attention."

"Ahh, there, you see, Lady Fraser? He has not left the palace, rather taking the time to care for his horse. A fine attribute that, don't you think?"

Lady Fraser came forward with an outstretched hand toward Alexander, and her daughter in tow with the other. "Aye, Your Majesty, a fine attribute indeed," she said with eyes locked on Alexander.

Politeness demanded he kiss her hand and allow her to introduce her daughter. He had to pull patience from his toes for this part of the day.

"My Lord, may I introduce my daughter, Lady Cora?" The woman shoved her daughter forward who looked equally as mortified as Alexander and, in that moment, he felt a slight bit of pity for the lass. Her eyes met his for a moment then cast down again.

"Are you enjoying the tournament?" Alexander asked her, hoping to put her at least a little at ease.

"Aye," she whispered.

"Do not forget you address an earl," her mother snapped at her.

"'Tis all right," Alexander said.

"Truly, 'tis not, my lord," Lady Fraser said. "The lass will apologize, now," she said and pinched her daughter.

The lass jumped and squeaked and said, "I am sorry, my lord, for my rudeness. I am enjoying the tournament very much. You rode very well earlier." With this she stood tall, and when he looked at her countenance, saw none of the earlier shyness, but rather a slight smirk on her face.

And this was the game, played over and over. A minor infraction at the beginning of an introduction draws in his attention and concern, then they jump into the compliments, all in an attempt to ensnare him. God in heaven, how much longer would he have to endure this farce? Maybe it was time to just marry someone and remove himself from the market. He envied the married men off to the side enjoying an ale and banter while he and any other untethered man in the hall had to endure this sort of madness.

He prayed that someone would come and save him from this insanity before he truly lost his mind and fell for one of them.

CHAPTER THREE

A T NO POINT in her life had she ever been so enthralled by God's creatures. For there had never been a time when she had seen so much of his creation in one place. Marion listened to the queen as she described each and every animal in her possession. Marion found herself drawn to one very colorful bird with a long, elegant neck, beautiful blue-green plumage, and tailfeathers that fanned out to form an elaborate pattern finer than any tapestry or fabric she'd ever seen. The bird also possessed what looked like a crown of feathers that appeared to float above its head. Clearly, God had a finer hand with a needle and thread than any seamstress.

"Are they not the most glorious birds you have ever seen?"

"Aye, my lady. I am truly in awe of your collection, but surely God took extra time on these—what are they called?"

"They are called peacocks. And interestingly enough, it is the male who is donned so. The unfortunate female possesses no such bold colors and markings. For it is he who draws the attention of her," she said as she pointed to an all-white bird with the same shape, but looked like the artist had not yet set their palette to work.

Marion rather liked that concept and now had more admiration for the peahen. She approached the bird cautiously and crouched low, holding out her hand. The skittish peahen's head shifted back and forth a few times before inching forward and then placing its beak onto Marion's hand.

"She likes you, Lady Marion!"

The queen clapped her hands which spooked the bird who then opened her tail feathers for a moment, revealing a delightful spread of exquisite display before skittering off to hide behind a small bush. In her wake, she left a feather close to Marion who picked it up and stroked its soft shape.

"I have an idea, Lady Marion, if you will indulge me."

Marion stood with the feather still in hand, pleased beyond all belief she had been blessed by this bird's offering.

"Aye, my lady?"

"Ahh, there you are, my Queen," a deep voice said from the menagerie's entrance. "How fares your visit? And I see your new friend has a look of wonder about her that is quite pleasing. I take it you approve of my wife's pets?"

Marion curtseyed to the king and smiled at the kind look that passed between him and the queen. They might have an age between them, and which resulted in obvious challenges, but it appeared there was genuine affection present as well.

"She certainly does, my king," the queen said. "I believe I know how I shall dress her for this evening's masque."

Was she now becoming another of the queen's pets? Maybe, but somehow, she didn't mind for the day was turning out far more interesting than she could ever have imagined. And who could turn down a little pampering from a queen?

"Aye, Your Majesty. I am rather taken with all of these creatures. Truly, God's creativity is present in each and every one of them."

"God's creativity indeed," he said. "Well, I shall leave you both to it. I am taking Argyll for some sport. He is not the mingling sort, and I fear he may require a little saving from the eager mothers present this day."

He then kissed his wife on the cheek and left.

"Now there's a fine match, Lady Marion."

"Who do you mean, my lady?"

"The very eligible Earl of Argyll, of course. Did your mother not educate you on the nobles to most look for and those to avoid?"

Marion wished her conversations with her mother had been so productive. "I do not wish to speak ill of my mother, my lady, but she has been more interested in a marriage proposal for me than specifically from whom."

"Oh dear, well, that will not do. I shall tell you everything you need to know about all those present today. I have had a fascinating opportunity in this past year to observe the nobles and their families of this land, and I can tell you there is as much opportunistic intent here as there is in London."

Marion was relatively sure she understood what the queen meant, and her mother was a part of that mindset as well.

"Let us begin with the earl, shall we, Lady Marion?" the queen said as she linked arms with her, and they drew away from the menagerie.

They walked along the loch to where a beautiful garden spread out across its side. Finely ground stone crunched beneath their feet and the sweetest aroma filled the air as they drew closer to bushes of roses so full and so fragrant that Marion wondered if she had not just stepped into a living painting.

"His given name is Alexander Campbell, and he is one of the most sought after bachelors in the land. Are you certain you do not know of him already?"

"I confess, I do not, my lady. When my mother and father discuss such things, I usually try to be elsewhere or to not listen."

"I do understand. However, you do realize that with the right information, you can help them make a decision that is suitable for you."

Marion had not thought about it that way. Maybe there was something to be said for knowing more about the possibilities of who she may be forced to marry rather than going into it blind.

"Very well, my lady, you have convinced me to listen as you

tell me all about the eligible lords of whom I should and should not consider."

The queen laughed. "Now you're getting the idea. Right, back to Argyll. He is handsome, young, tall, has great means, and is one of the king's favorites."

"If he is all that, my lady, may I ask why he is not already married, or at least betrothed?" Marion could not help but ask the question. Was he a demon? Did he possess sores? If he was that perfect, surely, he would have been secured by now.

"You are too clever for your own good, Lady Marion. It is true, he is most eligible and would be quite the catch, but as the king said, he does not enjoy the engagement in society required to secure an equitable match. He claims he will marry on his own terms in his own time."

Marion rather admired him, for that was what she intended for herself as well. The difference, of course, being he was an earl and could do as he pleased.

"Very well, my lady, the earl is stubbornly single. Is there anyone else I should know about?"

"As far as who to consider, there are a couple in our presence including Lord John Stewart, the future Earl of Buchan. A fine young man who will grow into his attributes in time, but appears a bit of a shy one. Still better a man you can shape than one who will rule you."

Marion wasn't sure she wanted to shape or rule anyone. That was certainly not how she envisioned a marriage.

"Which brings me to my last note for you. Whatever you do, do not engage with Lord Ross. He is from the north, and though he plays the game well in our society, it is widely rumored he has orchestrated a group spin from the most recent Highland resistance still loyal to the former king and bent on unseating my husband. He is charming to a fault and will do everything to align himself with the king. I have singled you out this day for very genuine reasons and I am glad of them, but I fear that may also draw some additional attention to you."

"And what does this Lord Ross look like so that I may steer clear of him?"

"I believe you will know him as soon as you see him. There is something a little too polished, a little too smooth, and a little too flattering to believe anything he says."

Could that have been the black rider? Nay, 'twas not possible. The feelings instilled in her from their brief glances did not give her the impression of a false man. She had to know, but again needed to hold her interests close to her heart lest she find herself on the wrong side of the altar.

"I must ask, my lady. Did Lord Ross take part in the joust this morn?" She could kick herself now for not paying attention to the names when the riders were first announced. She would not make that mistake again and could see the benefit of arming herself with as much knowledge as she could about those gathered and their intentions.

"He was not in attendance this morning, Lady Marion. However, I did spy him at our repast."

Marion did not know if she should be pleased or concerned.

ALEXANDER WAS GRATEFUL for the escape offered by the king; however, now the man was bent on probing his impression of the ladies present. Would he get no peace this day?

"They are all lovely young ladies, Your Majesty, I am sure."

"I see through you, Argyll. Do not think I was not aware of your tight expression when I found you surrounded by the most eligible ladies in all of Scotland."

"I am grateful for the opportunity to meet them, Your Majesty, but I would rather get to know a lady rather than have her paraded before me, which I might add, is most uncomfortable for them as well."

"Well then, you shall enjoy this evening much more as no

one will know your identity." The king paused and sized up Alexander. "I trust you have brought something to wear for the masquerade?"

"Aye, Your Majesty. I have brought something to conceal my identity for the masque this eve."

They rode the remainder of the way back to the palace in relative silence. They had intended to hunt longer, but the black clouds looming over the rolling hills signaled the time to cut the trip short. They returned empty handed and parted ways. Alexander was more than relieved when Alain met him at the stables and directed him to an empty passageway toward his chamber. The palace was quite large and for this occasion, the royal couple made a portion of their apartments available to those who did not reside in the immediate proximity. It would take Alexander the better part of two days to return to Inverary Castle on Loch Fyne but that wouldn't be for another day. And he had to make it through this evening first.

Awaiting him in his chamber was his black and gold brocade tunic together with black trews and a black mask to conceal the top of his face, only revealing his mouth. He even brought a black leather belt to tie around his waist. If he was to suffer an evening of frivolity, he would do it in his own way.

Alexander sat in a chair near the open window and took advantage of the ale and food that Alain had put aside for him. Surely the king's cooks were the best anywhere. Alexander hadn't eaten since earlier, and this spread of meat and cheese and bread was most welcome and delicious.

Looking out over the loch, he thought about the night to come, and his thoughts drifted to the red-haired lass from earlier. So very different was she from the other ladies he'd met that afternoon, and he wondered why it was her mother hadn't partaken in the opportunity. Or maybe they had their sights on someone else.

He shook his head. All these games were so unnecessary when their fathers merely had to come together to discuss terms to secure a contract. The display was unnecessary. Alexander had some experience with women. At twenty-two, he couldn't be expected to have remained chaste, and he did want to like his future wife. So why did he dislike settings like this afternoon so much? He wasn't even sure he knew himself. But dislike them he did and this evening amid the flamboyance, he would be expected to dance and engage.

The setting sun cast long shadows across the stone floor. Alexander heaved a sigh and moved the bed to change into his festive attire. When he was nearly done, a knock sounded at the chamber door. Alain entered wearing a sideways grin.

"What has you in such mirth?"

"There is already plenty merry making had in the great hall. I am certain the level of costume will send your head into a spin."

"And you find that amusing? My head in a spin?"

"Somewhat," he said as his grin widened.

"Surely I can feign illness."

"No one would believe you. Now hurry up and put on your mask."

"I have an idea. Since you are so eager, why don't you wear my clothes and go in my stead?"

"Absolutely not, my friend. I would not trade places with you for all the marks in the king's treasury. Besides, I get to watch you squirm all evening, which will amuse me greatly."

"Some friend you are," Alexander said as he tied the black satin ribbon at the back of his head, securing his mask.

"We both know that if the situation were reversed, you would take just as much delight."

"I will get my revenge," Alexander said, now wearing his own grin.

They left the chamber and made their way down the narrow staircase, across the courtyard, and onward to the great hall. The sound of string and pipe musicians playing lively tunes was the first indication the masque was already in full swing.

Upon entering the great hall, he could not help but notice the additions since earlier that day. Thick floral garlands ran diagonally back and forth above the crowd. Long tables were adorned as well with floral arrangements and large platters of steaming meats, mounds of breads, and one very plump roasted boar. Tankards of ale and mead sat beside silver and gold goblets. Alexander was sure there was enough food to feed half of the country.

Gazing around, he could appreciate the effort the attendants had put into their costumes, and though he had paid good coin for his own, he almost felt underdressed.

"Do you dare enter into the thick of them?" a voice asked beside him.

Alexander would know him anywhere. Lord Ross was the only other man there taller than he and clearly did little to hide his identity, opting to wear a tall hat with thistles and roses adorning one side versus a mask like nearly everyone else.

"I see you are ready to partake," Alexander said. Ross was known for his eagerness with ladies.

"And why wouldn't I be? With such delights to explore. I'm surprised at you, Argyll. Any of these hens are yours for the plucking."

It was a little disappointing that Ross had identified him so quickly. But better to send the man off to set his own fortune than influence his by proximity. If Ross could so easily identify him, then surely others would as well, and he did not want to be seen as eager.

The hen comment, while crude, was not overall out of line. Many of the ladies wore dresses with larger than normal skirts, lower necklines, and great long feathers billowing from their ornate head pieces.

In that moment of his contemplation, a group of young ladies drew their attention to the two men. Ross immediately puffed up his chest and moved toward them, allowing Alexander to slip off to the side and out through a door that led to the back garden.

The evening air was cool and welcoming from the heat inside

the great hall. As he walked toward the garden, the sounds from inside the palace faded and a calming wave settled over him. He would return in time, but for this moment, he would enjoy the solitude.

That didn't last long. Footfalls on the stone walkway behind him signaled company. He turned to see the silhouette of a ballgown walking in his direction. This one wasn't wearing the large headdress like the others; rather, her hair was down. There was some light emanating from the palace so that she should be able to see him, though he was head to toe in black.

"Is it your wish to escape the madness inside the palace as well?"

She stopped abruptly as soon as he spoke, for it was clear now that she thought she was alone.

"I am sorry, my lord. I do not wish to interrupt your solitude."

Her voice was like silk on his skin. She was still several feet ahead of him and he could not yet see her face.

"What is your name?" he asked, taking a step closer. He couldn't help himself; there was something about the way she moved and the shape of her figure.

"I am Lady Marion Baird, my lord. Might I have the honor of your name before I return to the palace? I am unchaperoned at the moment as I did not expect anyone else to be out here."

Alexander closed the distance and stepped to the side so she would have to turn, allowing him to see her face.

When she did, he caught sight of flaming red hair falling in waves down across her shoulders. She wore a white mask that appeared to be made from bird feathers. Her gown was not as low cut across her breasts as the others inside, but he could detect the swell of firmness beneath, and his fingers curled with a sudden itch to touch them.

"I am Lord Alexander Campbell, my lady. It is a pleasure to meet you, and I assure you that you are quite safe with me." She was safe but, in his mind, he was already kissing her.

"Lord Campbell? The Earl of Argyll?"

The comment caught him off guard and sobered him. Was she out for his title too?

"The very one."

He couldn't help the cold tone in his voice. For a moment, he thought she was different than the others.

"That is a relief, my lord. I became friends with the queen today and she mentioned your name as a trustworthy person. For a moment, I was worried I had happened upon someone she had mentioned who is not so honorable."

Well, this was a surprise. "The queen mentioned me?"

"Aye, my lord. She said you are handsome and dislike gatherings such as these. It would appear we have that in common." She hesitated then, "I-I mean disliking the gatherings, not the handsome part. I cannot see your face and I do not think about myself as handsome, I-I mean…please excuse me."

With that, she walked toward the palace at a brisk pace, leaving him standing in the near dark with his jaw open.

A few heartbeats went by before his stunned brain restarted and he regained his senses enough to follow her.

By the time he reentered the great hall, she was nowhere to be seen. So, he decided to go to the source. Staying on the periphery of the crowd, he found the king and queen at their table at the head of the hall. They were seated and talking to one another and smiling.

"Ahh, Argyll! I wondered when you would make an appearance."

Was there even a point of him wearing a mask if everyone recognized him so easily?

Alexander bowed to them. "Aye, Your Majesty, I am here as I promised I would." Then, turning to the queen, he said, "You are looking very festive this evening, Your Majesty. I wonder if I may ask you a question."

She sat up a little straighter and glanced at her husband before saying, "Of course you may, my lord."

Her voice was quiet, and he had been in her company enough to know her to be a little reserved.

"You made a new friend today and I wonder if you might know where she is at the moment?"

The queen opened her mouth and then closed it quickly. A slow-forming smile rested on her lips.

"You have an interest in Lady Marion, Argyll?" the king asked.

Did he? Having followed her into the palace and now seeking information from the king, it would appear he did in fact have an interest in one Lady Marion. This realization was likely more surprising to himself than anyone else.

"I believe all you need to do, my lord, is turn around. She is standing right behind you, speaking with her parents."

Alexander turned around and caught the full sight of her. Time seemed to slow as she turned, and their gazes locked. His hair prickled at his nape and his heart thudded hard in his chest. She wore a dark-green tightly-fit brocade bodice that narrowed at her waist and then bloomed into a full skirt made from fabric that shimmered in the light. Her white mask covered most of her face, but he could still clearly see her striking green eyes and plump pink lips that he now wanted to taste.

The king's voice beside him jarred him back to the present moment.

"I see you have met the fair Lady Marion, Argyll," the king said.

"He has, Your Majesty," she said. Her silky voice drew him in again. "May I introduce my parents, Lord and Lady Baird. Father, Mother, this is Lord Campbell, Earl of Argyll."

"The pleasure is ours," her father said.

"I am pleased to meet you all and wonder if I might be permitted to ask your daughter to join me for a dance."

He said this while keeping his gaze decidedly on her and wanting to place his hands on her waist and draw her closer.

"Aye, my lord," her father said. "You may dance with her."

Alexander noted her father's eagerness. Maybe he was not wrong about the parents, but she was a different story.

"Lady Marion, will you dance with me?" he asked.

She nodded and smiled. "Aye, my lord, I will dance with you."

He reached for her hand and led her away from her parents and the royal couple. Warmth spread through him, and he placed his hand on her hip and held her hand in his. Her tiny hand burned where she touched his shoulder.

Alexander had felt plenty of attraction before and knew lust well enough, but whether it was the music and the atmosphere or maybe something in the ale, he was bewitched by this lass.

As they moved in time with the music, his mind raced with images of what he would like to do to her, how he would like to pleasure her and how often. But she was not a common lass. She was a lady and would be available only through marriage. The thought sobered him again. He was not ready for that kind of commitment with someone he had just met. His mind warred between his growing desire and his logic.

"I see trouble behind your eyes, my lord. Are you worried about the other dancers, or is the crowd becoming overwhelming again?"

So, in addition to enticing him to want to bed her, she possessed the uncanny ability to read his mind. He had better take a care, for otherwise, this wee lassie might very well have him tethered to her before the dance was over.

"I am not troubled, Lady Marion." He was such a liar. "I am enjoying the dance with you very much.

He must have sounded convincing, for a moment later she smiled, and he was lost in a sea of fantasies about her all over again.

CHAPTER FOUR

THE COMBINATION OF music, food, and mead were enough to fill Marion's senses to the brim. But they were nothing compared to the man who confidently swayed her body to the delightful string and pipe music surrounding them.

His eyes were the deepest shade of blue, the like of which she had never seen before. Having left the great hall what seemed like mere moments ago, Marion was startled by the deep voice that called to her in the garden. Her startle turned to something else once she spied the blue eyes behind the mask. Head to foot in black, she recognized the black rider almost immediately, though she did not know his name until he introduced himself. Her black rider and the queen's recommendation were one and the same, Alexander Campbell, Earl of Argyll. Not that the title mattered to her.

Truth be told, she wasn't sure much mattered to her while in his arms. She could feel thick muscle beneath his shirt as he moved them around the floor. His chest curved beneath his tunic, and she had to confess to herself she'd never taken such notice in a man before. But this man had caught her attention fully and completely. Her body hummed from his proximity, and though they were in a hall full of people, she could only see him, those eyes of his that seemed to look into her very soul. She was more alert now, she was certain, than at any other time in her life. He, all of him, captivated her and held her breathless for more of his piercing stare, his sensuous mouth, and his oh so delicious scent that was doing all sorts of new things to her insides.

"Now it is you who looks deep in thought, my lady."

Was she losing her wits or was there a slight emphasis on "my"? "I am well, my lord. I am enjoying the music and this dance."

"As am I," he said and leaned down a little closer to her. "I do hope you intend to stay for the remainder of the masque."

"I should hope to stay, aye, but that will be up to my parents to decide at what time we shall depart."

"And where is it you will go when you leave here?"

"We will return to our summer home here in Linlithgow. 'Tis not far from here. My father wished to be close to the palace in order to attend the king's events if invited."

"I suspect there will be more invitations extended to your father, Lady Marion."

That was an odd thing to say. "Why would you say that, my lord?"

He smiled. "I meant only that you stand out among your peers, Lady Marion. I anticipate your parents will want to be sure you are introduced to the king's court sufficiently in order to secure a future for you."

There it was. The disappointment in that every person here had an agenda, including this seemingly perfect man who had imprinted on her heart for a few mere moments.

Thankfully, the dance ended. Marion curtseyed before the earl. "I thank you for the dance, my lord. It was a pleasure to meet you." With that, she walked away from him before he could respond.

As she approached her parents who were still speaking with the royal couple, an arm encircled hers and to her surprise, Lady Cora Fraser, a lass close to her age, and someone Marion would not trust as far as she could throw her, was fawning over her dress and hair.

"I told my mama earlier I wanted to wear my hair down tonight like Lady Marion does, but she would not let me. She said it is wanton and wicked to make such a display of oneself."

Marion looked up to the tall bird fastened to the top of Cora's head with feathers seeming to shoot out of the poor creature. Display of oneself, indeed. Cora always had a way of complimenting and insulting a person in the same breath. Marion would have disentangled herself were she not in the presence of the king and queen. As far as anyone else present was concerned, she couldn't care less what they thought of her or her hair.

"You might think you are better than the rest of us, Marion, but you are not. And you had better forget about the earl as well. Two fathers already approached him this afternoon and began negotiations, and from what I am told, he is the worst sort of womanizer," she said in a smug tone. "I hear he is even worse than Lord Ross and merely wants to marry a woman to produce heirs and that he has declared he will never love anyone."

Marion had lost most of her patience by now. "Well then, it is a good thing I am not interested in the earl." As she said this, she withdrew her arm from Cora and moved to sit with the queen who had now moved back to the raised dais and was motioning for Marion to sit with her.

"You look troubled, my friend. Why are you not dancing with the earl?"

Marion did not want to lie to the queen, but she also did not want to be pressured into spending time with someone who played the same games everyone else in the hall played. Was there no one present who was genuine? Maybe she was naive like her younger sister kept saying. Maybe this is how the world was, and she had better find a way to get used to it and accept her fate.

"It is all a bit overwhelming, Your Majesty," she said, using the proper address considering they were within earshot of others at the moment. And she hadn't lied. She was overwhelmed, just not for the reason she would let the queen think.

"Then we shall sit here together and watch the games ensue."

Marion was grateful for her friend's good sense. She didn't probe her any further, and as they sat in silence, Marion was able to watch scenes unfolding before her, connections between lord and lady with their hopeful parents standing by the sidelines whispering to one another. A moment ago, she was among that ever moving crowd and she wondered who had been whispering about her.

Her eyes scanned the hall until they landed on the earl in a dance with another hopeful young lady. She watched as he moved with her around the dance floor like they had. While the lady stared only at him, Marion was convinced his head turned her way whenever possible.

She noticed her father moving toward her wearing a small frown. "Are you unwell, daughter?" he asked after bowing to the queen.

"Aye, 'tis been a long day, is all." It had been a long day, and she wanted nothing more than to get out of these clothes and crawl into her warm bed and sleep.

"I couldn't agree more. Your mother and I are ready to leave if you are."

"Would you mind terribly if we did leave soon, Your Majesty?"

The queen placed her hand on Marion's. "I have been far too demanding on you this day. In truth, I have enjoyed every moment we have spent together. Will you please return on the morrow for the remainder of the games?"

How on earth could she say no to that? "Aye, Your Majesty. It would be my honor to return tomorrow and share in the games with you."

With that, she stood and took her father's arm to collect her mother who was speaking with Lady Fraser. Marion groaned inwardly, for she could imagine the stories she would have to endure on the carriage ride home.

Together they bade their hosts farewell and promised to return early the next day. Keeping to the side of the hall, they passed by those still enjoying the music and Marion was careful not to scan the crowd for the earl.

But she didn't have to.

"Lady Marion, are you leaving?"

The sound of his voice made her belly flutter. She stopped and turned to him. "Aye, my lord. 'Tis been a long day."

"And do you plan to return tomorrow for the games?"

"Aye, my lord, we plan to attend," she said, noticing other couples turning in their direction as if to attempt to overhear.

"Are you aware of the tradition of a lady offering a favor to their preferred participant?"

Did he mean like the scarf the queen had tied to one of the player's spears?

"Aye, I am aware."

He smiled then, showing white perfect teeth. "Good. I shall see you on the morrow then."

He then turned on his heel and walked away from her in the direction of the royal couple.

Did that mean he wanted her to tie a scarf to his spear? She had no idea and had no one to ask. Of one thing she was very certain. As much as she needed it, sleep would evade her this night in place of images of a black knight with deep blue eyes to torment her.

"AM I DREAMING it or do you wear a smile?" the king asked Alexander as he approached the dais and sat beside him.

"I do not know what you mean, Your Majesty," Alexander said with a grin.

He could have kicked himself after she walked away from him. But if he was going to invest any of his interest in this lass, he had to know if she was different from the rest of them and not just because he wanted to bed her every which way he could think of to pleasure her.

He was not proud of himself for asking another lass to dance whose name he did not remember. But he had to confess, he did not quite know what to do with himself after she left him standing there. When the other lass approached him, he was grateful for the opportunity, though it was not fair to her for he had no interest in anyone other than Lady Marion.

A small part of him liked that she watched him the entire dance, and he hoped it was because she wished she was his partner.

He would see her again on the morrow. Would she bring a favor for him? Would she bring one for another? The thought didn't sit well with him, making him shift slightly in his seat.

"You are very distracted at the moment," the king said. "Have you heard a word I've been saying about tomorrow's games?"

"My apologies, Your Majesty. I am a little distracted. I am looking forward to the games tomorrow."

"I was talking about the order of procession prior to the games. I wish to have you ride out first."

"Me, Your Majesty?"

"Aye, you. You are the strongest participant and so should take the lead in the procession."

"If that is your wish, I will happily comply."

"It is my wish. Now tell me what distracts you," he said and looked around the hall. "I do not see you looking at anyone in particular, and so therefore I can only conclude you are pining for a certain red-haired lass."

If he admitted it now, there would be no end to the king's hounding for a betrothal, and Alexander wasn't sure enough of his own feelings on that matter to agree to anything. He was very much taken with her, and he was sure he would dream of her this night. But lust is fleeting. He'd barely had a conversation with her to know anything of her character. Nay, he would admit nothing this eve and rather reassess in the light of day.

"I am pining for a good night's sleep after a long day."

The king shook his head. "What is wrong with everyone wanting to leave early because they are tired. Very well, I release you to your chamber, but you will have no excuse for perfection at tomorrow's games."

"Aye, Your Majesty, that is a fair trade." To both royals, he said, "I thank you both for a bonnie evening and bid you both a good night."

With that, he bowed to them and walked toward the edge of the hall, praying no one stopped him along the way. By the time he reached the entrance to the courtyard, Alain was waiting for him and Alexander had already removed his mask and was rubbing his face.

Handing the mask to his friend, he asked, "How was your night?"

"Mine was nowhere near as interesting as yours appeared to be, my lord."

"Do not start with me, Alain, or you will be walking back to Inverary."

"Och, that's a pretty big threat. She must have really stolen your heart, then."

"Do you ever have anything else to do besides torment me?"

"But it is so much fun," he said with a chuckle. "But seriously, I will say one more thing only on the subject as I do feel you are sensitive on the topic."

"And what is that?"

"Of all the beautiful ladies who were in attendance this evening, some of the most eligible and lovely ladies in all of Scotland..."

"Aye?"

"You danced with the most stunning among them."

"I don't want you looking at her," Alexander said before reason could prevent him.

"I knew it!" Alain said. "You are taken with her. Well, this is wonderful news."

"There is no news to tell. I am not taken with anyone, and you will remember that you were going to say nothing more on the topic."

"Very well, I will say nothing more on the topic this night." Under his breath, he mumbled, "But tomorrow is another day."

"I heard that."

"I said nothing."

They walked in silence the rest of the way to Alexander's chamber. Once there, he asked, "I trust your accommodations are sufficient?"

"What, no nightcap to discuss tomorrow's games strategy?"

"Not this night. I plan to retire early and get some much needed sleep."

"Very well. Are you sure you are well?"

It was a fair question as Alain would be used to them staying up late and discussing all manner of topics. But Alexander was in no mood for such a night. He needed some peace and quiet to restore his energy.

"I am well, Alain. Go and enjoy your evening."

"I believe I shall. There is talk of a late jig with the kitchen staff once the hall quiets down."

"I am sure you will enjoy that. Good night, and I will see you on the morrow."

"Good night," Alain said and closed the chamber door.

Alexander heaved a sigh of relief as he released his belt and tossed his tunic, trews, and shift to the small clothes chest he'd brought with him. Standing naked in his chamber, he poured a goblet of ale and stood by the open window with his arm resting above his head on the frame. He stared out over the loch and beyond to where small lights twinkled from the houses on the other side. He wondered if Lady Marion was in one of them or if their house was farther down on the other side. Which was more likely as there were larger manor houses down there.

He sipped his ale as he watched the moonlight flicker and dance on the water. His mind was filled with images of her. How she felt in his arms, the bright intelligence in her eyes, even her scent was burned into his brain.

He thought back to when he'd first seen her earlier that day which now seemed like an age ago. She'd made bold eye contact with him then, the same way as this evening, but it did not have the same impression on him now that it did earlier. He'd taken her action as greed, but now he wondered if she was admiring him. The thought thrilled him. Could she possibly feel the same intense attraction for him as he did for her? Did young lasses feel that way? He had no idea. The way he wanted her right now was almost animalistic. Surely a refined young lady would not harbor feelings like that. Nay, 'twas not possible.

Alexander downed his ale and placed the goblet on the table. He moved to the bed and flicked back the bedding and crawled inside. The bed was large enough for him to be able to spread out and try to find a comfortable spot to relax. As he lay on his back staring up at the dark brocade fabric on the canopy above, his traitorous brain envisioned Marion sitting atop him, riding him hard. His loins tightened at the thought, so he turned to his side. A raging erection would not help him get closer to sleep, so he flicked the covers off as if anything touching his skin made his need grow.

"Damnit," he said as he got out of bed and poured himself another ale. He pulled a chair over by the window, hoping for a cool breeze to settle him down.

He tried to think of other things. Tomorrow's joust would not be overly challenging, but he would need to properly focus lest he land on his arse in front of everyone or worse! He thought about the work waiting for him back home and of his younger siblings. He thought about the workmanship the king had access to in order to pull off these grand affairs. He even wondered how the cooks prepared the bread in order to make the inside soft and chewy but the outside deliciously crusty. By and by, the ale and the cool air helped settle him enough to crawl back into bed. He wasn't sure of the hour, but he was hopeful he could manage at least a few short hours of sleep before the sun rose again. The last thing he saw in his mind before fading was a vision of Marion tying a handkerchief to his spear.

CHAPTER FIVE

To say her nerves were on edge would be a gross under-statement. Marion tucked a kerchief into the pocket of her skirt and left her chamber. She'd taken a little extra time with her hair this morn and had chosen a pale-green gown for the day's event which was of a lighter fabric to allow more comfort from the summer heat. She was particularly fond of this gown and its fine stitching along the edges. The sleeves were long, but not as heavy or floor length as the one she'd worn the day before or last eve.

She met her parents, sister, and two younger brothers to break their fast. This morning, their cook had prepared bread and cheese together with boiled eggs fresh from the hennery, and though her belly took the brunt of her nervousness, she managed to eat a healthy meal before heading out.

"I heard you up and milling about last eve, Marion," Alice said. "Did you not sleep well? Anything in particular on your mind?"

Nothing she would confess to her meddling sister for certain. "Nay, just overtired from the festivities, I would imagine."

"She might have had something to keep her occupied, had she not wanted to leave so early. Just when the earl had started to show an interest in her—"

"Now, now, wife. There's no need of stirring that up. She was tired and we came home and that is the end of it."

"The earl?" Alice asked. "What earl?"

"The Earl of Argyll, no less," her mother said.

Alice grinned. "Is he handsome?"

Marion was absolutely not about to answer, and she was grateful her mother also did not comment.

"He is handsome enough," her father said, "but more importantly, he is a good man with a good head on his shoulders. He has had the burden of looking after his family, along with the clan and the region for three years now, and he has done so admirably. You could do far worse than he."

"I am not doing anything with anyone. I am going to these events because you have forced me. I had one dance last eve, and you are already selecting wedding clothes. Please do not embarrass me today."

Marion wasn't sure she could take it if her parents really showed a greedy side in front of the earl or the royals. For good reason, she did not want any of them to think she was like that. There were certainly enough young ladies with marriage on their minds for everyone to leave her alone and in peace.

"No one will embarrass you, sweet daughter," her father said. He then looked at his wife who was practically pouting. "That much I promise you."

"Very well, I shall hold my tongue. But mark my words, the longer you are in a man's company, the more likely he will propose. And that is all I shall say on the subject. Now, if everyone is ready, we shall call for the carriage and make our way to the palace."

They rode to the palace, only making small talk about the day's events. The joust would commence first and then repast, and after that, the men were all invited to a boar hunt while the ladies would be offered a formal tour of the gardens and menagerie. Marion had seen both but was eager to learn more about the animals mostly, but from what she'd seen of the gardens, they were very elaborate. It appeared everything the king drew his attention to turned into the most incredible array of beauty and style.

The carriage stopped just inside the courtyard, and they exited and made their way again to the tournament area on the back of the castle by the loch. The queen smiled widely when she made eye contact with Marion and patted a seat next to her.

"How fare thee this morn, Lady Marion? Did you rest well?"

"Aye, that I did, Your Majesty. And you, did you rest well?"

"I did indeed. I do hope you are looking forward to today's schedule. I believe your earl is to lead the procession."

"He is not my earl," she said quietly.

"I believe he might think differently," she said in a low voice, thankfully, so that only Marion could hear.

"What makes you say that, Your Majesty?"

"A young lady's father has enquired after the earl who retired not long after you left, by the way. My husband told the father he was wasting his time and that the earl would not be interested in the man's daughter, for he had already formed designs on someone else."

"But you do not know that someone to be me, do you?"

"I do not know it for certain, but I did see how he looked at you last eve and how he held you while you danced."

"He danced with more than just me, though," Marion said. "It is possible he was referring to someone else."

"Would you like me to ask him?"

Marion was mortified at the thought. "No, please, I beg you do not."

The queen smiled. "Then no more talk of denial. The earl likes you, Marion. There is nothing wrong with allowing that to happen. Are you afraid of him?"

She shook her head. "I am not afraid of him. I am just not eager to be married off to a man I just met."

"Married off? No one is saying that. But there is no harm in allowing a man to get to know you and for you to get to know him to see if there is something there."

The queen did make sense. It would be easy to jump to conclusions based on her mother's vocal intentions. Marion didn't want to offer attention to anyone if she were not genuinely interested in them. So that was the question. Was she genuinely interested in the earl? She reached into her pocket and withdrew the kerchief she'd brought.

The queen caught sight of it and said, "I am pleased you have that with you. I expect that is for the earl?"

"Aye, but I do not know where to put it."

The queen chuckled softly. "You put it wherever you like. I placed one for my cousin before yesterday's joust. You may do so for today's. It can be tied to his spear or handed to him to tuck into his gauntlet. The choice is yours."

There was something rather naughty at the thought of tying the thing to his spear and so Marion knew what she would do if the opportunity presented itself. And she was not about to tell the queen the earl had encouraged her.

Silver horns blew their clear tones announcing the participants' entrance. Marion leaned forward to get a clearer view of them trotting in atop their horses in a singular line with a shining black-armored rider leading them.

She was nudged by the queen when the rider stopped before them and bowed to them. Marion's heart beat like a rapidly thumping hare as she stood and took the steps needed to greet the rider. His mouth was hidden behind his helmet, but his eyes were not, and they bore into hers as he raised not his arm, but his spear to her.

She drew a shaky breath as she slowly wrapped the kerchief around the tip of his spear and tied a double knot to secure it.

"I wish you luck, my lord," she said.

"And I thank you for your favor," he said. "You shall sit with me during today's repast, aye?"

She released a slow breath and nodded then smiled. "Aye, my lord. I will sit with you."

He then bowed to her and took his position among the participants who were in line to receive blessing from the king.

Marion sat as the king then stepped forward with much the same messaging as the day before. This time her eyes never left the black knight's as his never left hers.

The king's words were a blur to her as her senses seemed to heighten. She became keenly aware of every inch of him and let her mind drift back to their dance and how safe and right she felt in his arms. The muscular curvature of his breast plate was the exact shape of him and clearly was molded for him specifically. Marion's cheeks heated at the thought of seeing that chest bare. What would he feel like? A wave of his leather scent washed over her, giving her goosebumps on her arms. The spell was only broken when he had to move to the edge of the tournament area to take up his place for the first joust. As he passed by, she was certain he winked at her.

ALEXANDER WAS IN very real danger of becoming obsessed with the lass if he did not get himself together. Alain strapped his spear to his arm as Alexander got into position. Maybe it was a mistake in having Lady Marion tie her favor to his spear. He should have taken it from her and tucked it into his armor, for now, in lining up to best his opponent, he would not be able to miss it. And worse, he now couldn't very well remove it for fear of disappointing her.

"Are you unwell?" Alain asked with concern in his tone.

Alexander shook his head. "I am well." He blocked the lass from his thoughts and focused on the rider opposite him. Leaning forward, he waited for the flag to drop then kicked his heels into the horse's side and rode hard toward the rider. A split second before hitting the man in the chest with his spear, the kerchief moved over the top of the spear and an image of her lovely face floated before his eyes. The sight of it was enough to distract him so that his aim shifted, and he missed the rider. He was not so fortunate, for the rider had aimed to unseat Alexander and was successful since he was not hit.

With his balance displaced, he fell hard to the ground on his back, the wind leaving his body with a great woosh. His head snapped backward as his skull slammed against the back of his helmet. He closed his eyes as stars formed and the world spun about him.

"My lord!" Alain's voice was distant as Alexander tried to regain his bearings.

When he opened his eyes again, his helmet was off and both Alain and the king were staring down at him with a worried expression.

"Can you sit up?" the king asked.

Alexander rolled to his side and then attempted to sit up, but the dizziness in his head kept him going, so Alain caught him and kept him stationary. Thankfully the spinning settled quickly after that. Both men helped him to standing and onward to the palace. Inside, he was brought into a chamber and made to sit on the cot. Alain made to work removing his armor and gauntlets. Then removed his tunic and shirt underneath.

"My surgeon will be here momentarily," the king said. "It is important for you to tell us if you feel pain anywhere."

In truth, he felt pain pretty much everywhere, but for the king's purposes he understood what the man meant.

"It is my pride mostly. I do not feel as though I have broken anything."

"You gave us quite the fright, Argyll," the king said. "What happened?"

Alexander was almost too mortified to say. And even more now, realizing that Lady Marion would have seen the whole thing. But there was nothing he could do about it now. What was done was done. Maybe now he would be able to leave this mad place and return home. He made to stand, and when he did, the chamber spun all around him and he landed in a heap on the stone floor.

"That's it. You are to stay here until my surgeon gives you a thorough examination. Where on earth could he be?" With that, the king left the chamber, saying he would go in search of him.

"Seriously, Alexander, what happened?" Alain's tone was full of concern and carried none of the normal sarcasm and jest.

"Do you promise not to laugh?" he asked as he lay on the cot, barely able to look his friend in the eye.

"Aye, I am too concerned for you right now to find mirth in your explanation, whatever it may be."

"Very well then. I was distracted by the kerchief tied to the head of my spear that the wind must have changed so that it flew upwards and in my line of sight."

Alain's jaw dropped for a moment and then he closed it.

"Go ahead and say it," Alexander said. He was very well aware of Alain's enjoyment of a good jest and took delight in their misfortunes at regular intervals.

Tight-lipped, Alain said, "I promised you I would say nothing, and nothing I will say. I am only interested now in ensuring you are not permanently damaged, but I reserve the right to revisit the subject at a later date."

That was about as much as Alexander could hope for. He was certain he would have his ears full of Alain's jests but was grateful the man decided to keep it to himself for now.

The king returned with the surgeon in tow who set about to poke and prod every inch of Alexander, nodding and saying "mmmhmm" at various moments during his examination. Alexander remained horizontal for the first part of the exam, but with Alain's aid, he then sat as the surgeon put his ear to his chest and then his back.

This went on for what felt like an age, until the king, with hands on his hips, finally said, "Well, is he damaged?"

The surgeon then lifted Alexander's eyelids and looked into his eyes. He nodded then and turned to the king.

"He is not permanently damaged. But he has given himself a

good smack on the head and should not ride a horse for a sennight."

"A sennight?" Alexander asked. "That will not do. I must return to Inverary on the morrow as planned."

"You will do as my surgeon bids. I will send word to Inverary of your condition and you will remain here for the next several days until we are sure you are recovered." To Alain, he said, "Can you get him to his chamber, and I will have the maids heat water for a bath. No doubt the heat and steam will ease the ache such a fall will inevitably produce."

"Aye, Your Majesty, I can do that."

"Good," he said. To Alexander, "Go and rest, and if you feel up to it later, you will join us for our repast. Otherwise, I will have your man bring you a platter. If you need anything at all, you will let me know and it will be done."

There was no point in arguing with the king. Alexander knew better than that. He graciously accepted that he would not be leaving Linlithgow as originally planned.

Once the king and surgeon left, Alain helped Alexander to his feet and out through the courtyard toward the stairs toward his chamber. He was not one to become embarrassed easily, but with so many who would have witnessed the fall, he could not help but wonder about the resulting chatter.

But there was only one person's opinion he was concerned about, and as he reached the edge of the courtyard, she came into view. Having not reclothed himself. Alexander stood before her bare-chested.

"My lord, are you harmed?" she asked, her cheeks a flaming red.

"Naught but my pride, Lady Marion. I thank you for your concern." He noticed how her eyes flicked to his chest and back up again.

"He is to rest at the moment, Lady Marion," Alain said. "The king has insisted he remain here for a sennight. If you wish, I shall find you later and report on his wellbeing."

Alexander looked at his friend with raised eyebrows. Alain, true to his word, remained stoic and kept his eyes on her.

"I would like that very much, sir," she said.

"'Tis Alain," he said with a smile.

"Very well, Alain. I thank you and I do hope you are well, my lord," she said to him then curtseyed and walked back toward the tournament area.

"What are you up to?" he asked Alain.

"Naught, my lord," he said. "Now let us get you up these stairs before you collapse in front of all these people."

His words were enough motivation for Alexander to lean heavily on the man as they made their way up the stone steps. Once in the chamber, he fell on the bed and rolled to his side. His head pounded and his back ached. The king was right; he had not felt the full brunt of this accident yet and likely would not for a couple of days. It did make more sense for him to rest and be cared for than return to Inverary. Now with Lady Marion's concern, he was bent on recovering sooner as he would very much like to spend more time with her.

When he'd seen her just then, he could have sworn the worry in her face was genuine and matched that of Alain's. Maybe he looked more beat up than he realized, not that he was ever overly concerned with his own appearance in that regard, but he was concerned with good presentation and usually kept his appearance neat. That had all now gone out the window with any pride he might have kept if she'd not seen him half naked. He shook his head and buried it under a pillow and pushed thoughts of her and her opinion of him away before drifting into a heavy sleep.

CHAPTER SIX

WHICH HAD A greater effect on her, between the sight of him being thrown off the horse or his bare chest, she could not say. But the latter was an image she would not soon forget. Wearing neither his helmet nor his mask, their encounter was the first time she had seen his face and the descriptions of him had not been exaggerated. His deep-blue eyes and straight nose were accentuated perfectly by his sensual mouth. He was more handsome than a man should be permitted, and Marion was certain he was not a man who would be so easily forgotten.

Sitting with the queen again at the midday repast, she picked at her food. A part of her wanted to go to him and sit with him while he recovered, but she was very aware that would never be permitted.

"Our cooks will be disappointed if you do not at least try some of your meal, Lady Marion," the queen said. "You have seen he is not damaged in a permanent way and so you should take ease in that knowledge."

"I know you are right, Your Majesty, but I do feel responsible for the distraction, for I fear 'twas my kerchief that affected his line of sight."

"My lady, you cannot control the wind," she said, shaking her head. "It is a normal practice for a favor to be placed in such a location and so the accident was just that."

"Perhaps you are right," Marion said. "I have never seen a man fall like that, and I confess, I am still affected by the event."

"A fair statement to make. Come, let us begin our tour of the gardens. You have already seen the menagerie, and I want to show you my roses."

Marion followed the queen to the gardens and listened intently as she described all of the wonderfully blooming varieties of the woman's favorite flower. Row upon row of various colors and varieties demonstrated again that God was an artist at heart. The air was thick with the luscious floral scent enveloping them as they strolled through the garden for the next couple of hours.

Once they had seen and talked about nearly every flower there, they sat on a stone bench facing the palace. Marion marveled at the scope of the structure in its beautiful golden-yellow sandstone. There were too many carvings to count, but the favorite thing Marion liked about the place was how it overlooked the loch and its rolling hills beyond.

As she scanned the detail on the palace, she noticed a person looking out from a window high above them. She didn't have to think very hard to know who it was. The queen appeared distracted by a butterfly that had landed on a flower close by, leaving Marion to take in the man. Still shirtless, she let her mind drift to the memory of him standing before her, clutching his shirt and tunic when all she wanted to do was to wrap her arms around him to ensure he was unharmed. She closed her eyes briefly and when she opened them again, he was gone. She wondered if he was even there to begin with or if she was losing her wits.

"Do you see this?" the queen asked her.

Marion looked up to see a beautiful white butterfly perched on the woman's hand, opening and closing its wings slowly.

"Isn't she the most beautiful thing you have ever seen?"

"She is, my lady, but may I ask how you know 'tis a she?"

The queen looked at her with a quizzical expression. "Truthfully, I do not know. I just assume all butterflies are *shes* in the same way all wasps are *hes*," she said with a chuckle.

"Most wasps are hes," Marion said. "All except for the queen."

"And for that I am grateful to be a queen of people, not creatures with stingers."

Marion watched as the butterfly settled onto the queen's hand and ceased its movement. Male or female, it appeared to be content in its current location. Marion looked up just as a man exited the palace and appeared to be making a direct path toward them. She quickly recognized him as the man who was with the earl. He'd said he would update her on the earl's progress. Her belly tightened into a knot. She prayed the news was good.

"Good afternoon, Your Majesty and my lady. I have a message from the earl for Lady Marion if I may?"

"You may share your message," the queen said. "I trust it is not a private message?"

"No, Your Majesty, it is not a private message." To Marion, he said, "The earl would like to share his evening meal with you; however, he is not able to navigate the stairs and so the king has offered his solar as an appropriate place to dine. You will be chaperoned by myself and a maid of your choosing if you accept."

"I will provide an appropriate chaperone for her," the queen said. "And my husband is correct in that the solar is spacious and offers a beautiful view of the loch and the setting sun. What time did the earl wish to dine?"

"He said to leave that up to you, Your Majesty."

"And how did he know Lady Marion was with me?"

"He is able to see you from his chamber window, Your Majesty," Alain said.

So, she wasn't losing her mind. The thought of being alone with him even with a chaperone thrilled her to her core though evoked her nerves at the same time.

"Lady Marion? Will you accept the earl's invitation?"

"Aye, Alain, you may tell the earl I will accept his invitation. I shall inform my parents."

"And I will have a chamber prepared for you. There will be no need for you to keep your parents waiting or to travel after dark with all the potential dangers about. I shall handle everything," the queen said and walked off briskly, talking to herself and the butterfly that did not appear to want to leave her hand.

"Come, Lady Marion. I will escort you to your father."

Marion walked ahead of Alain and could not help but glance upward at the palace again. There he was standing in the window again, staring down at her. If her insides flip-flopped just from that notice, how on earth would she make it through an evening with his full attention on her?

She squared her shoulders and entered the courtyard and made her way to the great hall to where she had left her parents. When she entered the hall, the queen was already speaking with her parents and the king was off to the side conversing with some of his staff and a couple of guards. He waved his arms wide and motioned as if illustrating how something was to be carried.

"Ah, there you are, daughter. Her majesty tells me you have accepted a special invitation?"

"Aye, Father, I have if that meets with your approval."

"Indeed, it does," her mother said. "Her majesty said you are invited to stay here this evening, and we approve of that as well."

Her father gave her an apologetic smile. She supposed there was no reining in her mother now, and really, Marion had other things to fret about now like what was she expected to wear and if her day dress would suffice.

"Now you must bid your parents farewell, for we need to seek out the seamstress to alter a gown if necessary. We cannot have you dining with an earl in a daywear gown. You must look like a countess."

Marion surely did not know what a countess was supposed to look like, and she did not like to be overdone, but the look of delight in the queen's expression at the moment was such that she would not want to deny her new friend the joy she currently displayed.

Together they entered the queen's apartment, and Marion was immediately in awe of the adjoining chambers which included her large bed chamber, a sitting room overlooking the loch, and a bath chamber with a permanent copper tub at the center with privacy screens covered with beautiful tapestry depicting intertwining thistles and roses.

"I hope you like it. I have ordered a bath for you, and my ladies will help with your hair and to get you dressed."

"Your Majesty, you are too kind to me."

"It is the other way around, I assure you. It has been too long since I have had a companion, and I have enjoyed our time together tremendously over the past two days. Let me show you how grateful I am."

Marion raised her hands, conceding utter defeat against the woman's will. "Very well, Your Majesty, you may decorate me in any fashion you choose."

The queen clapped her hands and flashed a broad smile as she set about to command instructions to her maids and the men she had summoned to carry water for the tub. Before long, Marion was enveloped in steaming water scented with rosehip and lavender, and she could not recall a time when she was more fussed over in her life.

No detail was left unexplored, from her gown to her jewelry to the turn of the curls in her hair. Thankfully the queen did not want to put Marion's hair up and said some hair was ornament enough and did not need anything to take away from its beauty. The one thing she did insist upon was a wreath of spray roses and thistle blossoms.

When Marion was scrubbed from head to toe, her hair was then brushed and wrapped in pieces of cloth so as to let it dry into curls. As she sat for the maids, she wondered if the earl had been preparing in the same way or if she would be overdressed to share a mere meal.

Really, she was convinced he would be attractive in a sackcloth. Or better, nothing. Heat rose to her cheeks as she recalled his bare chest again. She would need to put herself in check if she was to conceal her attraction. She did not want to be perceived as wanton, but those were the exact desires she had for him. It was pointless to lie to herself.

Once her hair was dry, the maids removed the cloths and brushed her hair to a shine. Soft curls cascaded across her shoulders and her breasts. She was then moved into the dressing chamber where four gowns were hung on display.

"Your hair is glorious in this light," the queen said. "Now come and stand by each gown so we may determine which complements you best."

Marion knew immediately which she preferred, the pale-blue brocade bodice with the highest neckline stood out to her straightaway.

"I agree, the red does not suit you, though the claret you wore yesterday was lovely on you. Let me see you by the rose one, and no, not that one either." The third was a green gown but the color was almost murky, and Marion was certain it would not be flattering against her pale skin.

"Let me see you by the blue gown," the queen said and raised the fabric against Marion's hair and skin. "This one is perfect, and I have just the perfect accents for it.

With that, the queen left and the maids stripped off Marion's robe and began the task of assembling the pieces of her gown. First her shift, then her bodice, underskirts, then skirt, and finally the outer bodice. Marion was sure she wouldn't be able to sit down and nearly giggled to herself at the thought of eating standing up. By the time the queen returned with her jewels, Marion was standing before herself in a full-length mirror, wondering who that person was in the reflection, for she had never seen herself like this before. Truly, the effect was regal, and if that was what the queen had been working toward, she'd achieved it. Now she truly hoped the earl liked it as well.

ALEXANDER PACED AS he waited for Alain to return to inform him the solar was ready and he could at least go there and await Lady Marion. He'd been deep in thought earlier when he viewed her and the queen strolling through the gardens earlier and he knew he needed to see more of her. He constructed a plan and, with the king's blessing, spent the afternoon organizing a private meal for them. As the hour for their meal drew closer, Alexander became nervous for the first time in his life regarding a woman.

It was not that he didn't know what to do with a woman or even be around one of Marion's status. He wanted this encounter with her to be without all the cacophony of the great hall and all its guests as he desperately needed to know if she was, in fact, different than the rest. He would then let himself give in to the passions she stirred in him. And they ran deep. Alexander had tossed and turned the entire night thinking about her. There was the definite possibility his sleepless night played a role in his mishap earlier, for which thankfully the bath and a tonic from the surgeon had remedied.

Now as he waited for their evening to begin, he took one more glance in the full-length mirror. He'd opted to wear his dark blue brocade tunic with black trews and black boots. He didn't want to meet her all in black again, for certainly she would start thinking him a dark lord and that was the last thing he wanted.

If he had it his way, they would both wear their most casual attire, but he was well aware that with the king and queen's involvement, this would be a lavishly set meal, and he would honor them for it.

"It is ready, my lord," Alain said from the doorway of the chamber. The man's expression was somber as he wore a slight frown.

"Is aught amiss?" Alexander asked him.

"Nay, my lord. But you look like a prince and the lady looks like a princess, and I fear I will lose my best friend after this night."

Alexander shook his head. "No one will lose anything this night; of that I assure you."

Alain seemed to shake himself out of his musings and then stepped aside for Alexander to exit the chamber. They walked to the solar which was not far, just down the hallway and around a corner. The sight that met him when he entered caused him to draw in his breath.

In the span of a few short hours, what he assumed was a relatively undecorated solar where the king conducted his business much like his own, had been transformed into an extension of the lavish decoration in the great hall. A long table was dressed in beautiful floral arrangements and many platters of meats and cheeses and pies, along with ale and mead and red claret no doubt from the queen's stores.

Near the main window, a smaller table was dressed in a gold candelabra, gold goblets, and gold trenchers. Two men he assumed from the kitchen stood by the food and drink, and as he passed by heard Alain tell them to pour Alexander a goblet of ale.

As he took in the decorations, he heard a sound behind him and turned to see Lady Marion enter with one of the queen's ladies in waiting. His breath caught in his throat when he locked gazes with her.

She sparkled like a million diamonds between her shimmering pale blue dress, diamond earrings and necklace, and fine ribbon that danced through her hair from the floral wreath she wore on her head.

This dress, similar to the one she wore the night before, was modest in exposure around her breasts, but he could still make out their curvature and appreciate the shape of her waist.

He stepped toward her and extended his hand. "Will you join me, Lady Marion?"

"Aye, my lord, I shall."

She took his hand, and from the moment they touched, his

body hummed with heightened awareness of her.

"Would you like a goblet of the queen's claret?"

She smiled and he stopped for a moment to stare at her mouth. "Aye, my lord, I would like that very much, for she has raved about it since I have told her how much I enjoy the mead she had made, which thankfully is less potent. I understand this claret is less potent as well."

Alexander didn't know that, but it made sense. His own stores of ale and mead were oft known to bring a grown man to his knees after consuming too much. It made sense to modify brewing to accommodate those who enjoyed the taste, but not the effect.

He poured a goblet then motioned for her to join him at the table. He placed the goblet down and moved her chair for her to sit then adjusted.

"I am very grateful you accepted my invitation," he said, hoping to commence a conversation to avoid any awkwardness. Christ, why did he feel so nervous?

"And I am very pleased to see you recovered, my lord. Truly, watching you fall was something I do not wish to experience again."

Was she even aware of the double meaning of her words? He had no doubt falling for her and losing her would be far more painful than landing on his head or his arse.

"It is not something I am in the habit of doing, Lady Marion, I assure you," he said, trying to keep his tone light.

"May I confess something to you?" she asked, making his pulse quicken.

"Aye, you may."

"I feel responsible for your fall. I should have insisted my favor be tucked into your gauntlet like her majesty suggested."

"The fall had nothing to do with the position of your favor, Lady Marion," he said and reached into the side of his tunic. "I intend to keep your favor as a reminder of the honor from a beautiful lady," he said as he pulled the fabric out to show her.

He'd insisted Alain retrieve it as soon as he woke from his sleep earlier, and thankfully the man appeared to read his mind and had already done so.

Lady Marion's eyes went a little wide and her mouth formed a silent "oh".

"So, you see, Lady Marion, you will not be permitted to blame yourself for a split second mistake on my part that landed me where I did for my own carelessness."

She gave him a shy smile and took a sip of claret. She appeared distracted for a moment as she tasted and contemplated the drink, giving him an opportunity to take her in. By God, but she was glorious in every way. And he was in big trouble when it came to her, as she did indeed appear a genuinely sensible young woman.

"Do you like it?" he asked her after watching her swallow and take another sip.

"I am not certain. 'Tis not as favorable to me as the mead, but I do think I like it."

"You may have whatever you like, Lady Marion."

She paused mid sip and then placed the goblet on the table. "You are very kind, my lord. Everyone has told me you are a good man."

He wasn't sure where she was going with that, but he would not jump to the same conclusion as he had the night before. It was not unreasonable for her to want to find a husband, and thus far she had approached the endeavor differently than everyone else.

"I should be glad to hear my reputation is such," he said. "I have heard nothing but praise of you as well from your new friend."

"It has been wonderful getting to know her over these past two days," she said and cast her gaze out the window.

"Is aught the matter?"

She turned back to him with an almost sad expression. "I am not certain you are the person I should be having this conversation with, my lord."

"Lady Marion, you may tell me anything."

She sat back and placed her hands in her lap. "Very well," she said. "I look at the situation of the royal couple and see that it was an arrangement made for them by others. I am in a situation where I feel I will not be permitted to have a say in a decision that will shape my whole future."

Alexander knew exactly what she meant as he had narrowly escaped a similar situation before his father passed. That situation had ended in disaster, and he was determined for his own siblings to have a say in their futures.

"Your father would force his hand if you were not in agreement?"

"Nay, my father likely would not, but my mother can be very decided when opportunity presents itself."

Alexander knew her sentiments all too well. And so where would that leave them? He would have to be very certain of his intent with her before letting any attachment develop. Even this shared meal could be perceived as such. Aye, he would have to be very cautious where she was concerned, for both their sakes.

CHAPTER SEVEN

THE COMBINATION OF candlelight, wine, and delectable company made a lasting mark on Marion. She could see why ladies like Cora would become competitive over a man like Alexander Campbell. What would the woman think now that they had shared a meal together? Marion could only imagine.

"You appear lost in your thoughts, Lady Marion," he said in a quiet tone. It appeared he had become quiet as well as he sat back and watched her.

"I believe I am as full as an egg, my lord. I assure you my thoughts are pleasantly engaged."

The earl's eyes widened for a moment before narrowing. Had she said something wrong? Why did his brow knit?

"Will you sit with me by the window, my lady?"

The servants had situated a long padded bench by the largest of the windows so as to enjoy the view of the loch.

"I would like that very much, my lord."

"And would you like more wine?" he asked.

She'd had more than enough and feared her innermost private thoughts would be set free should she imbibe more.

"Nay, my lord. I have had my fill," she said and made her way to the bench.

He sat beside her with mere inches between them, so close that she looked around to discover their chaperones all purposefully looking the other way. When she turned back to him, he was staring at her with a peculiar look on his face. His eyes seemed even deeper in color and his lips were parted.

"You are an enchanting woman, Lady Marion. How many men have told you that?"

"How many? My lord, I am not in the habit of being in such proximity with men to tell me such things." What kind of question was that?

He shook his head. "Forgive me, I forget myself," he said and shifted slightly away from her.

What was wrong with him? "Are you unwell, my lord? Is your head causing you trouble?"

His jaw dropped a little and then he started to laugh, a deep low rumble that ended with him raking his hand through his hair.

"You are a surprise at every turn, Lady Marion. Do you know that?"

"I confess, my lord, I do not know your meaning. Have I said something amusing?"

"Not intentionally, I believe," he said. "Tell me about your family. Your interests. Tell me everything about you," he said as he leaned back, folded his arms across his chest, and stretched his long legs out as if settling in for a long conversation.

She hoped she wouldn't disappoint him. There really was not over much to tell of her sheltered life of seventeen summers.

"I have three younger siblings, my lord. My sister, Alice, is fifteen summers and thankfully not yet out into society, and I have twin brothers who are twelve summers."

"Twins? And why do you say your sister should not yet be out?"

"My sister has a very different temperament than me, my lord. She is very bold and confident."

"I would consider you to be bold and confident, considering you have dined alone with me this evening. You do not appear to be suffering from nerves."

If he only knew the half of it.

"I mean to say that she is more confident in what to say in certain situations."

"Like what?"

Why was he so interested in Marion's sister all of a sudden? Maybe he was looking for a confident wife. Marion didn't consider herself that at all and grew a little wary of his questions.

"My sister would not have waited to be asked to a dinner with a fine gentleman. She would ask him." Marion hoped that was a sufficient example for him.

"And you think me a fine gentleman?" he asked with a seemingly genuine smile.

"Aye, I have told you that others have referred to you as honorable." She paused and made a choice to be bold for once. "Are you trying to tell me that you are not?"

He unfolded his arm and leaned closer to her. "Are you aware that everything you say has a double meaning to it?" he asked. "I cannot tell if you know of the effect your words have on me."

Effect? What in the world was he talking about?

"My lord, I believe you should maybe retire, for I think your mind has become more muddled than you realized earlier. My words are not meant to be taken in any way other than how delivered. What else could I possibly mean by them?"

She truly did not know what he meant.

"Are you telling me you don't want me to kiss you?" he whispered mere inches from her face.

Marion's breath caught in her throat. How could he decipher that from her comments? She thought for a moment and then realized what he was saying. Did she want him to kiss her? Of course she did, but as a lady, she was not about to invite him.

"I—never said—"

A heartbeat later, his hand cupped the back of her head, and his lips closed over hers. Warm and sweet like the mead and ale he'd recently finished, his lips played with hers, making her blood pound in her ears and her nipples harden. He shifted closer and deepened the kiss, coaxing her mouth open to accept him. In that moment, as he tasted her, she knew what it was to connect with someone on a level she never knew existed. His tongue touched hers, causing her woman's core to tighten and release in the most delicious sensation. Marion reached for him, placing her hands on the back of his neck and pulled him closer. She wanted to taste more of him, and when she circled her tongue around his, he groaned deep in his throat, sending shivers through her. Her entire body was so finely in tune with his, she was sure they were now one body.

Marion let one hand slide down from his neck to his chest, adoring the curve and thickness of the muscle beneath his tunic. He broke the kiss then and stared hard into her eyes.

"You do not kiss like a maiden," he whispered.

The comment was like cold water doused over her. She sat back abruptly, her fingers touching her lips as if he had burned her.

"I am a maiden, my lord. And you have taken advantage of me," she whispered and stood so she could place the bench between them. "You have worked some kind of magic on me, and now you want to blame me for it."

The more she thought about it, the angrier she became. He was the one reading into her words to serve his lust. Well, he would work no more of his sorcery on her. Marion turned on her heel and made for the door.

"Lady Marion, do not leave, please," he said, his voice nearly hoarse. "I did not mean to offend you."

But it was too late. She was offended by his comment and mortified by the wanton behavior she had displayed despite promising herself she would not act on her own growing desires.

She turned to see him with his head down in his hands, his arms leaning on his knees. A moment of something close to empathy washed over her, but her anger won out.

"I thank you for your company this evening, my lord, and I bid thee good night."

She didn't wait for his answer, but rather left the solar and made her way to the chamber that had been made up for her. Once inside, she tugged at the ties attaching all her gown's pieces together. She'd dismissed the maids, not wanting them to see her upset, so she was left to struggle out of the damned thing herself.

After an age, she had managed to remove all the baubles and ornaments from her body and pulled a light silk shift over her head and crawled into bed. The material was cool against her heated skin from the wine and the gown and the company. Marion rolled to her side and shoved her arm under the pillow to help shape it under her head.

Damned man.

Why did he have to be so wonderful in one minute and so coarse in the next? Well, he could fall off as many horses as he pleased from now on. Marion would give him no more thought or attention. She would return to the manor house as early as possible at daybreak, even if she had to walk there herself.

Marion flicked the covers off and lay flat on her back, staring at the canopy above. She could still smell him on her, still taste him. Flipping herself to her other side, she tried to find a position that would allow her to find slumber and escape from the torment he'd caused. For many hours, she was quite unsuccessful.

How long he sat there with his head in his hands, he was not sure, but eventually, Alain cleared his throat.

"Can I get you aught, my lord?"

Alexander didn't trust himself to speak. He could hardly process what he was feeling, let alone what he might want. He stood and reached for the window ledge to steady himself then shook his head at Alain as he passed and headed to his own chamber.

Once inside, he sat on the edge of the bed with his hands

cupping his knees. He was an utter fool. What prompted him to question her after she so willingly opened to him, he didn't know. But he'd likely lost her in the process. Every part of him wanted her and he was convinced she wanted him as well.

So why did he misread her words to think there was intentional double meaning? But if that was the case and she hadn't been inviting him in, why did she not push him away when he kissed her?

There could be only one answer, and it was unlikely now he would have an opportunity to be sure. Nay, he needed to separate himself from this place. He couldn't think near her, and shy of being able to ride his horse himself, he would have Alain secure a carriage. They would leave straight away; even then it would take them two days to arrive home. But he could stay there no longer.

Alexander opened the chamber door to find Alain just outside.

"I decided to wait in case you changed your mind and needed something."

"Aye, I do. Speak with the king's steward and secure a carriage for us to leave straight away. We will need to take some of his men to assist us and one to ride my horse. I do not wish to delay."

"Will you send word to the king?"

"I will go to him now as I know where he spends his evenings."

Alain agreed and went to do as he was bid.

Shy of being in his solar, Alexander was aware the king enjoyed spending time in his library which was filled with manuscripts and scrolls from all over Europe. The man spoke six languages and prided himself on being exposed to as much of the world as possible.

Sure enough, when Alexander entered the library, the king was bent low over a scroll which was opened wide on a table and secured open with glass orbs.

"Your Majesty, may I have a word with you?"

The king looked up and smiled. "Your evening has ended so soon?"

"Aye, and I must beg your indulgence for a carriage as I must leave here as soon as 'tis secured. I know I cannot ride, but I feel I must make haste to Inverary."

"Is aught amiss?" the king asked and made his way to Alexander, motioning him to sit.

How he longed to stretch the truth and say he'd received word of a sick sibling, but this man deserved better of him.

"I believe I may have misjudged and ultimately insulted Lady Marion. I do not wish to offer details and beg you not to force them from me. But I cannot think here. My mind is muddled, and I need the security of my own home to clear my head. I plead with you to release me."

The king sat back and regarded Alexander. His brow knit and his mouth turned into a frown. "I will grant you this, Argyll. But I expect to see you again before this summer has ended either here at Linlithgow or by invitation to Inverary."

His relief was great as he let out a heavy sigh. "I thank you, Your Majesty, and aye, I have been planning an invitation for you and your wife since your marriage last year. If you let me leave now without fuss, you shall pick the date, and we shall have another grand fete in your honor."

This news brought a smile to the king's face. "Then you shall travel within the hour and in my most comfortable carriage. I will have my footmen accompany you and my best guard to return your horse."

"Thank you, Your Majesty. This is a great relief to me," Alexander said and stood to bow and leave.

"One more thing," the king said.

Alexander held his breath and waited.

"Regarding Lady Marion. Do I need to offer any apologies to her family on your behalf?"

The meaning was quite clear and thankfully, the encounter

had not advanced to that level. "Nay, Your Majesty. She is intact."

The king looked surprised for a moment before masking his expression. "Very well, I bid you a safe journey and I will send word of our anticipated arrival date.

Alexander bowed and left the library. He was careful there were no servants or anyone else in the hallway before heading to his chamber. Alain was packing his belongings when he entered.

"Did you speak with the king?"

"Aye, he has agreed to release us this eve in a carriage with the assistance of his footmen. He's offered his own guard to ride my horse, but I would rather you rode him. We shall have to stop somewhere tomorrow eve, but we can make that decision then. How long before we are ready?"

"We can leave here as soon as the footmen come to collect your chest. The steward will have the kitchens wrap up some food and libations for us to take with us."

Minutes later, the footmen arrived, and Alain directed them to the trunks. He waited for them to leave before asking, "Do you need assistance with the stairs, my lord?"

Alexander shook his head and left the chamber, not looking back and not really looking around until he entered the courtyard and entered the awaiting carriage. He took only notice of the lavishness and comfort he would have on this ride, but was less pleased with the additional time the trip would take. Nevertheless, the sooner he was away, the better.

He closed the curtains to the windows and leaned his head back. God's teeth, what a mess he'd made of things. On the seat opposite him was a wineskin and a basket. Not that he was hungry, but he did appreciate the drink and hoped it was ale. He opened it and took a swig just as the carriage was pulled forward. Maybe between the gentle rocking of the carriage and the beverage, he would find a way to settle down.

But every time he closed his eyes, her face came into view and every time he took another swig of ale, 'twas she he tasted. He was certain he would go stark raving mad stuck in the carriage on his own for the next several hours, and so he knocked on the roof for the driver to stop. Be damned, he would not sit in this box alone. When the carriage stopped, he stepped out and spoke to one of the extra guards who had accompanied them but had no current role. Minutes later, the guard rode his horse, and Alain was sitting on the seat across from him, grinning from ear to ear.

"If I have to endure this unnecessary luxury, then you will too," Alexander said.

"I am not complaining, my lord. For I have always wanted to be cavorted about the country like a lady. I believe the only thing I'm missing is a low-cut gown and plump breasts."

"I have enough visions in my mind's eye I wish to forget at the moment. I do not need to have one more, particularly one that is quite disturbing."

"I am pleased at least that you did not insist on riding your horse," Alain said. "I know you are troubled, and I know how private you are with your affairs, but if you wish to talk about what happened this evening, I am here to listen. I was in the solar so I do have a sense of it, but we all moved as far away as we could, and I made sure the staff were farther away than me."

"Do you think the maids will talk?" He hadn't thought about that. Damn, but he was a daft fool for he had likely put her reputation at risk.

"I do not think anyone will say a word. And I know this because I did hear the queen speaking to them ahead of the dinner that their discretion was expected."

At least it appeared the queen had hand-picked the maids. Alexander, while grateful for the company, was not much in the mood for chatter and so resealed the wine skin and tossed it to Alain then let his head fall back, praying for the chaos in his mind to release.

CHAPTER EIGHT

STILL WRAPPED IN the quilt she'd pulled from the bed, Marion woke in the chair she'd pulled over by the fire hours ago. She stared into it before finally dozing. His mind and body and heart warred with the other throughout the night. And at the end of it all, she came to the same conclusion she'd had from the beginning; she would return to her home this morning, but she would wait until she could at least thank the queen for her hospitality and move on with her remaining time here.

Her family had planned to stay at Linlithgow for a fortnight; however, maybe she could convince them to return to Posso Tower where she could become lost in her dreams once again among the rolling hills and fall asleep under the ancient oak trees.

But that was not likely now she had been noticed by all. The queen had assured her of discretion among the staff so she was not concerned the intimacy would have been viewed by anyone else. Even now, hours later, her skin burned where he'd touched her, and her body tightened and pulsed at the memory of being so possessed and then rising to that possession with her own demands.

Marion shook off the quilt and moved to look out the window over the loch. Dawn had broken a while ago and the early morning dew had not yet burned off the grass nor the light fog hanging just above the water. This was the time when the night and morning met for a few moments before the one gave way to the other, as if the dew and fog hung on long enough to tell the sun of the events of the night before.

How long she stood there, she did not know. Finally, a knock at her chamber door roused her from her musings.

She turned as two maids entered with steaming buckets and, seeing her state of undress and out of bed, called to the doorway, "Wait!"

One placed her bucket down and attended the fire while the other wrapped Marion in a quilt and urged her toward the fire before ushering in two men with a copper tub who placed it in the center of the chamber then retreated.

What followed was a flurry of maids with buckets of water until the bath was full and the scent of roses and lavender which now reminded her of the woman she was the day before versus the one she was today.

Marion lay in the bath as long as she dared. Two in a row was a luxury indeed, for she was not accustomed to such frequency but grinned, thinking she could certainly get used to the way the heat and scent tantalized and relaxed her.

By the time she was ready to get out, her fingertips had begun to shrivel. She let the maids do whatever they wanted with her and by the time they were done, her hair had been curled and brushed and she was dressed in a pale blush pink gown that surprisingly did not object to her red hair and fair skin, rather drew them together. The neckline was square, to which a sheer scarf was tucked for modesty, and the sleeves came only to her wrists. This gown was delicate and pretty, but sensible.

"Her majesty wishes you to join her to break your fast this morn, my lady."

"Oh," Marion said. She'd not been aware anyone had been awaiting her company and now felt a little mortified over her indulgence.

"When you are ready, my lady," the maid said.

Marion followed her out of the chamber and onward to the

queen's chambers and beyond to a lovely situated open and airy part of their apartments she had not yet seen. The largest of all from what she could gather, this one had a large hearth with highbacked padded seats surrounding it and a long dining table to one side, and smaller tables with lower backed chairs surrounding them. She found the queen seated at the long table with a large spread of food before her.

"Come and join me, Lady Marion. I do apologize that I could not wait for you. I found myself quite ravenous this morn."

Her butler motioned Marion to a chair to the side of the queen and then proceeded to offer food from each of the platters in turn. Not over hungry herself, but not wanting to cause offense, she accepted some cheese and bread and a few pieces of apple and orange slices. This morning, she stuck to the sweet mead. No more claret for her.

"How fared your night?" the queen asked.

The woman wasted no time beating about and thankfully did not wear any kind of smirk, for which Marion was thankful, for she was in no mood to be played with.

"You had outdone yourself, Your Majesty. The solar was beautifully decorated and the food and drink were the best I've ever had."

"And the night overall? How did that go, if I may be so bold?"

Marion reminded herself that this woman had not yet had relations with her husband and would not for some weeks according to the contract. A few things were becoming clearer to her in the light of day and now she felt even more foolish for falling into it.

"My night overall was lovely, Your Majesty."

"And you are to give me no details, then?"

Well, this was more awkward than she could have imagined. She didn't want to disappoint her friend, but she was not about to talk about how the man's kiss had turned her insides to mush, and the driving need to touch his bare skin in ways she wasn't sure she would be permitted.

"We had a lovely dinner; as I said, the food was heavenly. After that, we sat by the window and watched the moon's reflection on the loch and we talked, or rather, I talked. He wanted to know about my family and the things I was interested in."

"And then?"

If she already knew and Marion did not confess to it, that would be lying to one's queen and Marion was not about to do it.

"What do you mean, Your Majesty?"

She cleared her throat and leaned closer. In a lower voice, she asked, "Did he kiss you?"

Marion closed her eyes. God in heaven, give her strength. "Aye, Your Majesty, he kissed me, but that was it, a very brief thing that I do not wish known."

The queen tilted her head to the side. "I also get the sense you do not wish it repeated."

"Nay, I do not. I was hoping to return to my parents this morn."

Her friend's eyes narrowed. She sat back in her chair and interlaced her fingers with her elbows on the chair's armrests and her two forefingers raised to a point placed directly beneath her chin.

"There are two things I want to ask you, and I want you to be very honest with me. My reasons are my own for asking them, but I absolutely guarantee you discretion. The maids who attended you, who acted as chaperone last eve are my most trusted, but they are loyal to me. I know what happened. So, the first question is, did you enjoy the kiss?"

Caught off guard by the woman's blunt question, she blurted, "Aye," before she could catch herself.

The queen now smiled as if satisfied with that answer.

"Very well, that is what I would have expected. The second question I have for you is if you enjoyed the kiss, and by all accounts, as did the earl, why did he leave here in the middle of the night?"

"The earl has left?"

Marion's heart sank to the floor. This she did not know, and though she had fully intended to avoid him at all costs as she made her own escape, at least she managed to stay the rest of the night before seeking to leave.

"He has returned to Inverary Castle which is his home."

She was not sure if she should be relieved or if she would lose the little food she had just consumed.

"I see this news troubles you and I do not wish to upset you. If it is your wish to return to your parents, I shall call for the carriage straight away. But know this, my friend," she said in a gentle tone, "you will not leave this place with any guilt over these past days. You and I have struck a friendship that is only beginning, and I will take great care in your wellbeing."

"I thank you, Your Majesty. I do wish to return home and I am very grateful for your fellowship and your kindness. Truly, it has been a singular moment in my life I will not soon forget."

That seemed to satisfy the queen enough that she waved to the butler and gave instructions for Marion's safe passage to the manor house where her parents no doubt waited for news of a betrothal. What in the world was she to tell them?

THERE WAS NO place like home. A common conception, but that sentiment was no truer to Alexander than it was in the moment the carriage pulled up the drive and Alain roused him with the announcement they were home.

He stretched and scrubbed his hand down across his face then exited the carriage without a word to anyone. It was still very early in the morning and so there were few people about, so he made his way straight to his chamber, stripped off his clothes, and crawled into his bed. Sleep hit him hard and fast as if he'd not slept in an eon.

The sun was high in the sky when he woke again, momentarily unaware of his surroundings with a pounding in his head. He sat up and looked around him. His trunks had been brought up, but not unpacked, and a tray of food and tankard had been placed on a table by the fire. The day was cooler than those he'd experienced at Linlithgow and so someone had also lit a fire which was welcome.

He pulled on his trews and leine and tunic and made his way to the food. Whether it was the relief of being home or the extra sleep, he couldn't be sure, but he was ravenous. First things first. He would eat then go see his sister. He wanted to ensure a nice quiet evening meal with his family, and since she was not expecting him, he was not sure if she'd had anything specific planned. He was in the mood for meat and lots of it.

He finished his meal and took advantage of the water basin and cloth left for him to freshen himself. He then left his chamber to see who was about.

Finding them in the great hall, he was delighted when his youngest sister, Cora, ran to him. He picked her up and raised her high above his head before swinging her around, immediately regretting it as the hall spun for a moment, and he then placed her on the stone floor.

"We did not expect you so soon, brother," his eldest sister Jean said. "Alain has told me of your accident. Truly, you look like a dung heap."

Kissing her on the cheek, he said, "You are always my biggest flatterer, sister. I thank you for keeping my feet firmly planted on the ground."

"Come and join us. Have you eaten?"

"I have, but wanted to ask you about the evening meal. Have you planned it yet?"

"I have ordered mackerel. Your ghillie should be leaving here shortly."

"Call him back. Has the cook any wild boar? Rabbit pies?"

"Well, someone has an appetite. I will go see what I can do, and when I return, you will tell me all about your time in the king's fancy palace."

"I want to know about the fancy palace too!" Cora said as she jumped up and down.

"Aye, little one, I will tell you all about it. Did you know the king owns a lion?"

"What is a lion?"

"Don't you say another word until I've returned from the kitchen," Jean said and rushed off.

Putting his hands up in defeat, he said, "All right, I won't say another word."

Alexander took his seat at the head of the table and kissed the top of her head when Cora crawled into his lap. She had always been possessive of him and particularly in the three years since their father's death. Now at eight summers, she would soon lose interest in her older brother and find other interests. For now, he would accept her attention. He watched his younger brothers fight with their wooden swords while Thomas, at nineteen, was trying to prove he would make a good master and instructed them in their swordplay. At nineteen, at least he was not making trouble in which he excelled.

He and Thomas had had their moments since their father's passing. Thomas, who had always been headstrong, would prove difficult when it came to being patient and appropriately planning for their futures. He was more interested in the drink and games of chance he found in the local taverns than settling down. He now had the responsibility of helping to raise siblings, particularly after their mother died, followed by their father five years later.

Little Cora was his biggest worry. She had never known her mother and barely knew her father before he too left this world. It was no wonder she clung to him and Jean so much. But before long, Jean would be married off as well. Within a year, he was determined to find her a suitable match, though he would miss her quick wit and impeccable ability to run a household.

"It is all sorted," she said upon her return. "The cook had

already put a boar on a spit last eve for he'd been planning for that upon your return, but he said it will be done for this evening if you wish."

Alexander did wish. He wanted nothing more than to enjoy the peace and quiet of his home with his siblings by his side all safe and sound.

"Now will you tell us all about the palace?" Cora asked from his lap.

"Aye, little one. What do you wish to learn about first?"

She looked at him with wide eyes, for how could she know what a palace looked like, or those things contained within?

"Very well, let me tell you about his animals."

"And can you tell us about the beautiful lords and ladies?"

"Aye, sweet one, I shall."

Alexander spent the next hour describing in as much detail as he could muster between their endless questions.

"Did you dance, brother?" Jean asked.

"Did you? Did you?" Cora asked.

"Aye, I danced with two ladies."

"And were they beautiful?" Cora asked.

"Aye, they were beautiful." One whose face would be burned into his mind for all time, he was certain.

"Why do you look sad?" Cora asked.

"I am not sad. I will miss the palace," he said, which was only a small lie.

"I wish I could see the palace and the king and queen," Cora said.

"Well, maybe you can."

"What does that mean?" Jean asked. "We cannot all travel to Linlithgow Palace."

"Nay, we cannot, but the king wishes to visit us here at Inverary before the summer is out. What do you say to that?"

Jean's eyes widened for a few moments before a broad grin spread across her face. "The king wishes to visit us here?"

"Aye, very much so, and he wishes to bring his new wife who

is just a little younger than you, sister. I know from my visit that the queen enjoys the company of other ladies close to her age." He prayed none of them would probe on that subject.

"It would appear I have much planning to do," she said. "We will have to move you out of the master's chambers."

"Aye, that is satisfactory. Those chambers are too much for me, in any case."

"I will happily take up residence in them," Thomas said.

"Nay, you will not," Alexander said, shaking his head. The lad knew no boundaries.

"If I meet a queen, will that make me a princess?" Cora asked.

"Nay, my sweet. You are Lady Cora and that you shall remain until you marry a lord when you are much older."

"How does one prepare for a visit from a royal couple?" Jean asked with what appeared a question more to herself than anyone present.

"I believe one consults with her brother, the cook, our steward, the ghillies, and house staff to formulate a plan. This king enjoys grand affairs with no expense spared. Maybe we can show him what a quieter, more peaceful existence looks like."

"But will I get to stay up late and dance?"

"You will have a dance and a new gown, I promise," he said.

"When do you want this to happen?" Jean asked.

"I will send word for them to join us in three weeks."

That meant he had a lot to do in a short time, but at least it would keep his mind off a particular lady.

CHAPTER NINE

THE DAYS BLED into one another as Marion's parents carted her around from one social gathering to another, and though she tried to smile and be polite, her heart was not in it. While she did appreciate the solitude in the evenings with her parents, she had hoped to hear from the queen by now. The queen's parting words rolled over in her mind like crashing waves on a beach. An agenda had been present the whole time, of that Marion was certain. She could not entirely fault the queen for wanting to know more about a subject of which no one would speak in front of her. But still, Marion would have a care in the future when dealing with people in more powerful positions than she. She would be far more attentive to what was happening around her.

Just when she'd given up hope, an invitation had come from her majesty. In it, she was cordially invited to the midday meal with the queen in her apartments. She would be collected by the king's guard shortly before. That gave Marion little time to select a gown and make herself ready.

She didn't have to think long to decide which gown to wear, for the gowns her mother had ordered upon arrival at Linlithgow had arrived the day before. In the selection was a soft lavender one with soft edges and butterflies stitched into the delicate, multi-layered, nearly sheer fabric. Marion had been itching for a reason to don it and this would be the perfect occasion.

Having seen all the young ladies with their fancy head dress over the past weeks, Marion had worn hers down but was in a different mood today. She spoke with her maid and was pleased when the lass agreed emphatically. What resulted was a loose pin up with curled tresses hanging down the sides and some on the back. Her hair was so thick that it looked like she had added more once her maid had finished pinning it all. She was very pleased and insisted tiny hawthorn blossoms be added all around to finish the effect. Between the butterflies and flowers, Marion was sure she looked like the queen's garden had spat her out.

Before long she was whisked away to the palace in an ornate carriage with her father in tow who had been invited to the king's afternoon hunt. Once there, they separated and bid the other a fond day. Marion followed the servants to the same hall where she'd last seen her friend whom she hoped would be pleased to see her.

"My dear Lady Marion," she said upon her entry. Her expression was pleasant and genuine. "I have missed your company. Do come and sit with me for I have much news to share."

"Your Majesty, I have missed your company as well."

They sat at the table which was, as usual, adorned with elaborate floral arrangements and more food than one could consume in a week.

"Pray tell me what you have been doing since we last met? I confess, I have been consumed with entertaining my husband's endless rotation of guests. It seems the man requires his days to be filled with entertainment."

The queen prattled on for a spell about the various dignitaries from Italy, France, and Spain who had come to see the impressive Linlithgow Palace and all its glory, and her husband was all too ready and willing at any point to exhibit.

"Listen to me, asking you a question and not giving you a chance to answer it."

She stopped talking and paused, giving Marion her cue. While nowhere near as exciting as the queen's account, Marion told of strolls along the loch with her family and dinners with other families in the area. She told of her brother falling from a tree and breaking his leg which she was not sure her mother would survive. Aye, her mother who wailed day and night at the need for the culprit tree to be destroyed. All in all, it had been busy, but quiet.

"You could use some distraction, I believe, Lady Marion."

If it was anything like the last time, Marion would pass. She'd had quite enough of that kind of excitement for a while.

"What do you mean?"

"I have an invitation to discuss with you."

"Aye, Your Majesty?"

"My husband and I plan to tour the west Highlands and will be leaving Linlithgow in some days." She paused for a moment then continued, "I would like you to be my companion. We will be gone for a few weeks to return before the summer is fully out. What do you say? Will you join us?"

Marion wasn't sure how to react. 'Twas not like anything she'd ever done. Besides Edinburgh and Linlithgow, she'd only been to her home, and she had always wondered about the much acclaimed west Highlands.

"I must ask my parents," she said, having quite easily made up her mind to accept.

"No need. My husband will speak of it to your father on their hunt this day."

The queen had thought of everything as usual. There was only one thing left to discern.

"And which places shall we visit, Your Majesty?" It might be a bold question. She should be grateful to be invited at all, let alone as personal friend of the queen. But her curiosity was piqued, for she had been of the understanding that the royal couple would spend the entire season at Linlithgow, hence why her father had moved the family part and parcel to their manor there.

"That will depend upon my husband, but we have had one

very specific invitation I feel you will find amusing."

"Aye, Your Majesty? I do not believe I know anyone who lives in the west Highlands."

"Your memory is short then, Lady Marion, for our first destination will be that of Inverary Castle which is the home of the Earl of Argyll. I know it has been some weeks, but I do believe you would remember him."

The queen's attempt at jest was ill favored, though Marion attempted to mask it. What did she remember of the earl? Besides the mortification she still harbored over their parting, there was yearning for his company, his affection, his kisses. She was conflicted at every turn when thoughts of him entered her mind, and they had quite frequently since their parting. There had not been many nights when the torment of her encounter with him had not played upon her mind.

"Aye, I remember him. And is he aware you are inviting me to his home?"

"He is aware," she said. Was there a "but" in her tone somewhere?

"Your Majesty, I will not go to the man's home if he does not want me there."

"It does not really work that way, Lady Marion. The invitation has been extended to the king and those he chooses to invite as accompaniment. Our steward will send along the number of our party, but it is not customary to highlight those in the party as it is at the king's discretion."

Now she felt like a fool for asking. Of course, the king and the earl would not discuss her specifically, for who was she in this mix?

"You worry for no reason, Lady Marion. You will be very welcome, I am sure. And as for the other matter, I am sure it is long forgotten."

Which would be worse? That he did remember and did not want her there, or that he'd forgotten the encounter entirely. Both, by her estimation. But was that enough for her to turn down the invitation? She'd been longing for an escape from her family and here was one beyond her imagining. To travel across the country in a comfortable carriage with the queen to insist upon their needs and wants was not an offer that came along every day. Any other young lady would have said "aye" already. So why did Marion hesitate? The reason was obvious, and the only sensible response was as well.

"Then I will gladly accept your invitation, Your Majesty, and I will enjoy the adventure of it with you."

The queen's smile was infectious. "I do hope you like to be pampered, Lady Marion, for I've had our carriage fitted with extra padding and footrests that pull out from under our seats for added comfort. We shall want for nothing and see all the sights there are to see. I assure you, this will be a journey you will not soon forget."

Of that, Marion was fairly certain, regardless of her encounter with the earl. The queen shared some of their intended itinerary including a stay at Stirling Castle. It would take them about a sennight to travel to Inverary, but they could choose to delay that should they become distracted along the way.

The remainder of their visit was taken up with the clothing Marion should pack and the shoes and wraps she would need since the air may very well be cooler in that part of the country versus the Lothian region.

All of that was well and good, but Marion wanted to know more about Inverary and the earl and his family and everything she could imagine. Instead of asking, she paid close attention to everything the queen shared with her by way of preparation for the trip.

The earl.

She longed to see him again but dreaded it at the same time. Having mulled over his words time and again, she could not be quite sure of his meaning that evening. Did he mean she was merely pretending to be a maiden and using her feminine ways to ensnare him? Or did he mean some other such manner of insult? She was not experienced in the ways of men and women, but she was sure the need she felt was real, and she was convinced at least he had felt the same in the moment.

While she could understand being cautious with such attachments, she'd given him no reason to believe she was anything but truthful and sincere in her attention to him. Maybe something good could come from this encounter. She could very well acquire the opportunity to confront him over his comments. She could tell him how that made her feel and that she deserved an apology. The likelihood of that was as possible as if she might sprout wings and fly across the country to acquire said apology.

Keeping her mind focused on preparing for the journey was a welcome distraction from the memory of the man at the end of it. He would not know she was in the attending party. How would he react to seeing her? Would he think she orchestrated this as well?

ALEXANDER STRAIGHTENED HIS tunic and fixed his belt placement and left his chamber to join his family to welcome the royal couple to Inverary Castle. His sister had left no detail to chance as she'd driven everyone in the castle mad in the last two weeks since receiving confirmation from the king of their stay and the number in their party.

There was nothing unusual about the number and it was not customary for the king to provide details on the who. But two words stuck out that had him on edge.

My Dear Argyll,

I graciously accept your invitation to join you at Inverary together with my wife and friend as well as the usual accompaniment of staff. We shall endeavor to arrive on or about 18 August and will partake of your hospitality for a few days as we tour the west Highlands.

James S

Did the king mean his wife was also his friend, and if so, what a peculiar manner to phrase such a thing. If that was not the meaning, was it that the queen was bringing a friend, and if so, which one? Images of red hair had tormented him to no end of late, and he had just begun to work through possibly never seeing her again. Now he was not sure if he wanted to see her or not.

Alexander stood at the front of the line including first his family, then his stewards and heads of his staff. The din of an approaching carriage and horses was well evident long before the party came into view considering the curvature in the road and the lush trees surrounding it.

The king was at the lead and galloped ahead when they came into view. He dismounted quickly and tossed the reins to a waiting stable hand and approached Alexander with a beaming smile.

"Argyll, you seek to outdo me with these grounds," he said.

The king clearly had an affectionate eye for meticulously groomed grounds looking neat as a pin. Jean could be thanked for that. Not that a hair was ever out of place at Inverary, but she was specific about how she wanted the first impression to be taken. In addition to the lush trees that surrounded them, she'd had the gardeners gather branches from nearby to make thick garlands adorned with all the local wildflowers of the area. These garlands lined the entrance to the castle and topped every main doorway and table possible inside. His home smelled more like the woods than it did. But he was proud of his home and stood a little taller before the king as he bowed.

"You are most welcome, Your Majesty. I am certain you will find much to admire in this part of the country."

As the king spoke of his journey, the carriage pulled up and stopped just in front of them. Alexander worked hard to keep his attention on him, but in his periphery, he was keenly aware of the carriage door slowly opening and an ornately dressed foot stepping outside. The woman wore a hood and a gown fit for a queen—making sense considering that's who it was. She looked all around and seemed pleased then joined her husband in greeting Alexander.

He waited. His mind was having a different conversation with himself than the polite one he was having with the royals.

And then another foot protruded from the carriage, this one not so ornate, but a lady's foot just the same. Another foot and a rustle of pale blue fabric and a flash of red hair and he stopped talking mid-sentence. How much time passed as he watched her straighten her hair and gown, he was not sure, but somewhere in his consciousness he was aware the king turned to look in the same direction.

"Argyll," he said. "Do you remember Lady Marion from Stobo in Peebleshire?"

"Aye, I recall," he said as she drew nearer.

"She is here by invitation of my wife. I trust that meets with your approval?"

"Aye, Your Majesty, I do not object."

Their eyes met and the world fell away for a heartbeat. She was more lovely than he remembered. Something was different. Like she had been let in on some secret only she knew and it emanated confidence around her.

"Welcome to Inverary, Lady Marion," he said.

"I thank you, my lord," she said. "You have exquisite grounds, my lord. Your gardeners must be busy day and night to keep up such beauty."

Alexander smiled. He was pleased by her approval. Aye, there was something different about her, but he couldn't quite put his finger on what it was.

"And who is this lovely young lady?" the king asked, moving down the line to Jean.

Alexander spent the next while introducing his family and main staff to the king and their party. He stood closest to Marion during this time, drinking in her scent, fingers itching to touch her hair.

Her hair.

That's what it was. She wasn't wearing it fully down like when he'd first met her. Rather, she had some pieces loose but the majority of it was pinned up in large curls. It took a lot of restraint to keep from picking up one of the loose tresses and bringing it to his nose to inhale. Once or twice, she looked back at him over her shoulder and when she turned back, he would focus on the curvature of her neck, how he longed to press his lips there.

Once the introductions were complete, Jean pretty much took over guiding them through the castle and speaking of its long history of Clan Campbell and the short history of Inverary Castle.

"You've done well with your earldom, Argyll," the king tossed over his shoulder from time to time.

Marion and the queen had linked arms during the tour as the king asked question after question about the land and the sea loch adjacent to the castle and even questions about the Campbells' involvement at Bannockburn. By the time Jean was done with the tour, Alexander was filled with pride for the ease with which she had conducted herself before the royals, but also of the message she conveyed. They would never forget to honor all those who were loyal who had come before them.

Jean led them to the great hall where a feast was laid out which was not on the king's scale, but it was on their scale. They'd prepared various fish as the main for their midday meal and had reserved roasted boar for later that evening. Breads and other cured meats and cheese along with cold rabbit pies and more pastries than they could eat in a lifetime. Alexander had been the one to suggest the pipes play outside the castle during the meal which was something they reserved for only very special occasions.

At the table, the king and queen sat at the head with Alexander and Marion seated across from one another, with the remainder of Alexander's siblings filling up the remainder of the seats on either side as their ages dictated. Up to this point,

Alexander had not had the opportunity to speak with Marion but hoped he could manage to steal a moment or two of her time as the afternoon allowed.

"What of the sport in the area?" the king asked.

Thomas, who had been relatively quiet to this point, spoke up. "We've been tracking a particularly large buck for the past few weeks, Your Majesty. We would be honored if you would join us."

The king's eyes grew wide and for good reason. Alexander was well aware the king had been craving the opportunity to collect that particular trophy, and Alexander would see it happen as long as the animal was appropriately honored with no wastage of the spoils. In fact, if it were to transpire, Alexander would ensure the nearby village was invited to pay respects as they did when any of the majestic beasts were felled.

"I would very much like that. When do we leave?"

"We can leave within the hour, Your Majesty, if that pleases you," Thomas said.

"Argyll, will you join us?" the king asked.

"I beg you to excuse me as I have some things to attend to at the moment," he said as he pointedly caught Marion's gaze, "and it is my brother here who is the master huntsman. I believe he also has hopes to show you our best fishing places as well."

"Very well, if the ladies will excuse us," he said and arose from the table, "I believe I have a buck to collect."

With that, he kissed his wife's cheek and followed Thomas out of the hall.

"Your Majesty," Jean said. "Would you like to join me on a tour of the back gardens? I have heard so much about yours at Linlithgow. For surely ours are not so grand, but we have some very pretty places to enjoy the sun's warmth and the many songbirds visiting this time of year."

Alexander caught her eye, understanding what she was about. It appeared the queen did as well for she accepted very quickly.

"Lady Marion, would you like to see our library?" Alexander asked.

Her eyes grew wide for a moment. "Aye, my lord, I would like that very much indeed."

The younger siblings scattered about playing with their wooden swords again as Alexander offered his arm to Marion.

Her small hand clung to his arm lightly, but the sensation of it still brought a warmth that spread through him. If they were to spend the next days under the same roof, he would have to be sure they could do so cordially and without awkwardness. He didn't want that for either of them.

"I was quite surprised and pleased to see you earlier, Lady Marion, for I was not aware you were the friend the queen intended to bring."

"I apologize for that," she said. "I had asked her majesty to share that information, but she assured me 'twas not necessary."

"'Tis of no matter. You are here now, and we shall make the most of it."

CHAPTER TEN

WHAT IN HEAVEN'S name did he mean by that? And why did everything he said need interpretation? She needn't dwell on it long, for as soon as they entered the library, her attentions were duly captivated elsewhere. Not an overly large room, and nowhere near the volumes possessed by the king, still his library was beautifully structured with dark polished wooden shelves, some of which contained leather-bound books while a good many others were filled with scrolls of various thickness.

Along one whole wall was a large arched window looking out over the gardens and the loch beyond. She envisioned she could spend many happy days in this room exploring the material here. She'd only had some exposure to the written word, but at the king's behest, it was not considered fashionable to keep volumes of legends and knowledge in one's home.

Besides a beautifully crafted copy of the Bible, Marion had only ever seen a collection of Chaucer's works and *The Book of the City of Ladies* by Christine de Pizan. She concentrated on the understanding written word provided versus spoken and found she much preferred it.

Stroking her hand along the beautiful shelves, she started a little when his deep voice interrupted her thoughts.

"Do you approve, Lady Marion?"

She turned to him and hoped her expression conveyed just

how much she did approve. Before she could say so, he closed the distance between them and reached high above her to select something. It was only for a second, but the sight of his massive chest in front of her sent all sorts of mad visions into her mind's eye. A bare chest in the courtyard, feeling muscles flexing beneath her hands, the masterful way he moved their bodies around the dance floor.

"Lady Marion, are you unwell?" he asked.

The heat that had quickly risen to her cheeks told her that her thoughts translated to dangerous transparency.

"Aye, my lord, I am very well," she said. "Tell me what you have there," she said, hoping to change the subject.

He gave her a quizzical look then drew her to a table with high-backed chairs, drawing one out for her.

"These have been in my family for many years," he said as he placed three leather-bound books before her. "They contain some of the stories of our clan and this region which were transcribed by a monk from Iona who had decided his life's journey was to take him away from that place's sad history. He stayed with my grandfather for many years learning of this place and its histories and mysteries. During his time here, he transcribed some of them as a thank you. As you can see," he said as he opened one of the manuscripts to the first page, "his work was exquisite. 'Tis written in old Scots and Gaelic, but I have learned most of it along the way and am hoping if the king's commission works, I shall have this copied for safekeeping."

The work was incredible. Some pages contained flowing lettering while others contained illustrated depictions of beautiful maidens, fairies, and even sea serpents. This was the sort of volume that interested her.

She looked at him and asked, "My lord, what is the commission you speak of?"

Alexander explained that the king wanted a printing press established in Scotland for all its great works to be copied and made widely available not only to the nobles, but to commonfolk as well. It was some sort of device that would allow paper to be placed over inked letters and then dried, over and over until all the pages in a book could be cut, sorted, and bound.

Marion could hardly wrap her mind around it and the man before her who, without all the chaos at the palace, was much more at ease in this setting, and if she were to be brutally truthful to herself, so was she.

"I confess, I could spend much time in this room with all these stories to explore," she said, her mind thinking of far off lands, but perfectly content in the place she was and the company she currently kept.

"Aye, 'tis my favorite room in the castle as well. In fact, Lady Marion," he said as if an idea had just come to him, "when I was a wee lad, my father would invite an elder from the village just beyond those hills who would come to recite these stories to us and then give us their meaning. He still spoke old Scots and Gaelic and would keep us entertained for hours. Would you like that?"

The tone in his voice when he spoke of the man and the far off time was so compelling she could not help but watch his mouth as he spoke. His eyes grew darker when she replied, "Aye, I would like that, my lord."

For a few moments, neither of them spoke. Servants had been coming and going throughout the afternoon to stoke the fire or set aside libations on a side table, but at this moment, the library was empty save for the two of them.

Seated together and turned toward one another staring hard at the other, Marion was unsure what to do next. In the same way as at the palace, she became transfixed with him, unable to tear her gaze away.

Alexander leaned toward her, and she did the same. "Marion," he whispered and cupped her face with his hands, stroking her lips with his thumbs. Seconds later, he did so with his lips, sending shivers through her.

"Are you cold?" he asked. "Come, let us sit by the hearth." He drew her to standing and, taking her hand, led her to the hearth which provided warmth she didn't really need.

"Nay, my lord. I am quite warm," she said, which drew his gaze onto hers.

"I never know if you want me to kiss you or not."

Though it was chivalrous of him to apparently give her the choice, she wasn't quite sure what she was supposed to do, so she did what she wanted to do. Marion reached up with one hand and pulled him toward her until their mouths were a breath apart. She gazed into his eyes with as much courage as she could muster to let him see what she felt.

Alexander's hands were in her hair and at her waist, pulling her in as his mouth pressed against hers. Their tongues found a familiar dance as her hands entangled in his hair, attempting to draw him even closer than was possible. Alexander broke the kiss and tilted her head back then traced sensuous kisses along her neck while his hand left her waist and reached up to cup her breast. When he squeezed, she gasped, the sound of which was quickly buried by his mouth closing over hers again. Marion was becoming slowly consumed by his passion and hers and the growing need to know more of this man and the liquid fire that pulsed through her veins every time he touched her.

"God, I want you," he said as his mouth trailed across her cheek to her ear and down her neck again.

Aye, she wanted him too, but she was not about to admit it, and then the reality of their proximity and the fact that anyone could walk through the door, which she hadn't noticed had been closed, washed over her.

"My lord, we cannot," she said and stepped back from him.

His eyes were heavy with passion and his sensual smile was filled with the promise of all the delights Marion could imagine and more, considering she didn't know very much about such things.

"I will let you go, Lady Marion, as long as you admit one thing to me," he said in a tantalizingly steady voice.

"And what is that?" she asked as his eyes trailed the length of her, resting mostly on her mouth and breasts.

Meeting her gaze again, he closed the distance between them and brought his mouth to within an inch of hers. She couldn't help but part hers, ready and wanting the next onslaught.

"You will tell me you want me as much as I want you."

It was torture to say words like that to a lady of her years and status. Why would he want to make her voice it?

"Or else?" she dared ask.

His deep voice rumbled in a low growl-chuckle sort of sound.

"Or I will never kiss you again."

What choice did she have? She was never good at being un-truthful and doubted her muddled mind.

"I want you," she whispered.

Alexander's gaze fixed on her. He reached for her hand and raised it to his lips and kissed.

"Then I shall let it be known that I wish to court you," he said and promptly left the library and Marion standing there with her jaw agape.

HE MUST BE a madman to have said such a thing without first establishing she'd had no formal attachment to anyone else. But he could not help himself. She had to be his for there was no way he could ever stand by and see her with another man.

Alexander met the queen and his sister on his way out of the castle.

"You will find Lady Marion in the library, Your Majesty, sister. See she is entertained while I catch up with the hunting party."

He didn't wait to see if they agreed; rather he made his way to the stable to where his horse waited and whinnied when he saw his master approaching.

"Not so fast," Angus, the master stable hand, said. "Where do you think you're going, m'lord?"

Alexander had always given Angus way to speak freely, but in this moment, he needed to see the king.

"Angus, I know you're looking out for my well-being," he said with a sigh, "but it has been quite some time since my fall." It was an age at least. Alexander pulled his horse from its stall and mounted. "I plan to find the king and my brother on an important matter."

The old man's eyes narrowed. "You've the look of a woman's influence about you."

"A woman's influence?" Surely that was an odd comment to make considering Alexander was donned in his usual trews, shirt, and tunic.

"Aye, m'lord. Someone has caught your eye, and I can see she has made you frantic which is not in your nature."

"You are too wise for your own good, Angus," he said before kicking his heels and taking off out of the stable. He rode hard up the lane leading to the main road west. His brother had been tracking this buck for quite some time, and he wondered if today was the day he would be successful, or rather allow the king to be successful. Not that the man was without skill. Aye, he was well skilled in battle, but on the hunt was another matter indeed, for patience was the greatest virtue one possessed on the hunt, not strength.

After riding for what seemed like hours, Alexander found the men near a copse of trees standing in a circle and looking down. He approached them and dismounted.

"What goes here?" he asked.

"Brother," Thomas turned with bright red cheeks. "The most incredible thing." He moved aside to reveal the fallen buck. "He just stood there as if knowing his fate and did not run at all."

"He submitted to his king as he should have," the king said with a satisfied look on his face.

Alexander checked the animal who was for certain no longer

of this earthly world and noted the single arrow into its chest and clean slit across its throat. He placed his hand on the animal's forequarter and when he did, all the other men found a place on the animal's body to do the same. Eventually, the king placed his hand there too.

"Thank you for your sacrifice, old hart. You will be honored." Then to the king, he said, "You have your prize, Your Majesty. Are you pleased?"

Alexander was not overly pleased. For why should this creature be slain because it had survived all others of his kind and risen to the admiration of its kin? The animal should have been left to roam as he saw fit.

"Aye, that I am, Argyll. I thank you for this gift and am now indebted to you."

Not for long.

"Is there any favor I may bestow upon you?"

Alexander could think of only one thing. "I wish to formally court Lady Marion," he said.

The king's brow knit. "If you like the lass so much, why not marry her outright?"

"Because her father is not here to ask, and her family is not here to witness it."

"But I can approve it," he said.

Sometimes there was such a thing as too much progress. While Alexander admired the king's interest in spreading the written word to the masses and inviting philosophers and astrologers to court, some traditions were worth keeping, and Alexander would not begin any sort of relationship with Marion without her family's formal consent. What would be appropriate considering his encounter with her family at Linlithgow was a formal courtship.

"I thank you, Your Majesty; however, I wish only to court her until such time as I can speak with her father directly."

"Very well, Argyll. But take it from me, the long way around is not always easy. You have my blessing to court Lady Marion."

"Thank you, Your Majesty."

CHAPTER ELEVEN

MARION WAS SEATED by the fire when the queen and Alexander's sister entered the library. She had already straightened her gown and hair, but she was certain she was somewhat disheveled. Or maybe that was her insides. The madness coursing through her veins left her uncentered like a ship adrift at sea and seeking something with which to tether.

"Lady Marion, are you unwell?" the queen asked. The two women sat with her, both wearing concerned expressions. "The earl, while tearing off, told us to see to you."

See to her? She wasn't ill by any stretch of the imagination and she was not about to tell them his kisses had turned her insides to jelly.

"I assure you both, I am quite well. Maybe his lordship merely wanted me to have some company." Or maybe she wanted company different than his to distract and help process just what was happening to her.

She'd been around women who had become newly involved in an amour and had never viewed anyone seeming to possess masking or managing these types of feelings. Either they didn't feel them, or they were very good at hiding them.

"Very well," Lady Jean said, "I shall have refreshments brought to the great hall if you like."

"Lady Jean, might we take our refreshments in here?" There

was something quite comforting about this place. Like it had a welcoming and easy presence.

"Aye, my lady," she said. "I am pleased you like our wee collection. 'Twas my mother's favorite place in the whole castle, bless her."

"I can see why," Marion said. She liked the room, and she liked Lady Jean. The woman knew a great deal about the history of her clan and her pride shone through in her every action.

They chatted for a while as Jean described the portraits on the walls as well as the tapestries that had been handed down. She explained Inverary had only been around for less than half a century, but they'd worked hard to preserve the family's heirlooms and treasures.

"My brother is the second Earl of Argyll," she said. "The title was passed to Alexander upon our father's passing three years ago and with the blessing of his majesty. We are grateful for the honor and the support of Your Majesties. We have worked hard to protect these lands and her people."

Lady Jean was very passionate about her family, causing Marion to pause. Did she know half of her lineage? She'd been so caught up over the past years of fighting against her parents' aspirations for her, she had lost sight of her own histories somehow. Upon her return, she would surely rectify that and ensure Alice did as well.

The afternoon passed in pleasant exchange as the three shared stories of their families and their thoughts on social gatherings. It turned out, the queen preferred quiet evenings, but her husband was never happy unless the house was full, as it were.

Marion could see how a social gathering here could be full of people, but also not chaotic like the king's court tended to be. And she wouldn't have long to find out for there was just such a gathering planned.

"'Twill be quite different from your lavish affairs, Your Majesty," Lady Jean said. "We will have country dancing and storytelling, but the food will be decadent, that much I can promise."

"I welcome the change, Lady Jean, and thank you for your hospitality. Truly, these woods and these grounds are so very serene, I am certain the most troubled soul could find solace here."

And that was it. The point Marion could not find up to now. There was something about the way the castle was situated and surrounded, almost enveloped in beautiful foliage and trees, that whispered, "safe place." Even though the feelings the earl drew from her were somewhat alarming as they were so new, she was never in danger. Everything about that man also whispered the same thing.

"The men have returned, and they've killed the buck!" one of Lady Jean's younger brothers called from the doorway. He was a bit young for formalities, but he still stopped and moved to the queen and bowed his head then ran off.

Lady Jean looked to the queen who smiled and nodded then stood. "Ladies, shall we take ourselves to greet the men?"

"Aye, that we shall," Lady Jean said and directed them through the hallway and exited the castle.

Marion was not prepared for the sight that awaited. While she could not see the animal clearly for it had been wrapped in great canvas to protect it from the heavy drizzle, its size was unexpected. She'd never seen a buck, but didn't expect this great protrusion above the relatively large cart that carried it off to the area of the butchery and kitchen.

"Congratulations on your kill, husband," the queen said.

He dismounted and kissed her on the forehead. "'Tis the second most joyous thing I have ever done in my life."

Anyone who had eyes would have understood his meaning. It was obvious the king possessed affection for his wife. Marion admired that. That was how a marriage should be, and it had been long since she'd viewed such in her parents.

A light touch of her elbow made her jump, though she didn't

have to guess who it was.

"Lady Marion, might we take a walk in the gardens?"

She looked up to see the earl staring down at her. In this light, his eyes were so blue she was certain even the ripest blueberry would be green. How could she resist him and why would she want to?

"Aye, my lord. I would like that."

He tucked her hand in the crook of his arm and led her down the stone path that led to the gardens separating the castle and Loch Fyne. For long moments, neither spoke, giving her time to take in the serenity and peacefulness of a place where the loudest activity was the seagulls fighting over a fish.

"Do you like my home, Lady Marion?"

"Aye, my lord. 'Tis a beautiful place and is peaceful which reminds me of my home, though I do not have a loch at the edge of our lands."

"Posso Tower, is it?"

"Aye."

"Tell me about it."

"Well, 'tis not as grand as Linlithgow Palace, nor as large as Inverary Castle, but 'tis peaceful like here with rolling hills and quiet save for the creatures who share the land."

They lost sight of the castle as they strolled through the hedges and bushes of beautifully bloomed hawthorne, bunches of heather, spreads of bluebells, and yellow daisies. Truly, it was like they'd tamed the wild and groomed it to appear domesticated.

"Aye, I believe I too found Linlithgow Palace to be a wee too boisterous." He turned to her then. "Lady Marion, there is something I wish to ask you."

"Aye, my lord?"

They stopped and faced one another. He took her hands in his and raised them to his lips.

"I have a passion for you, Lady Marion, that has a need to be unleashed."

"My lord, I—"

"Nay, please let me finish," he said as he released her hands and raked his hand through his hair then turned from her for a moment. Turning back, he said, "I do not wish to dishonor you or your family, but my need to be near you increases by the second, and I cannot imagine you finding someone else."

He looked like he was in pain. Marion moved to him and placed her hand on his cheek. "My lord, what ails you?"

His hands were around her waist in an instant as his lips claimed hers. She opened to him as she wrapped her arms around his neck and pressed her body against his. She had no capacity for restraint like earlier. She wanted him, every part of him touching her in every way.

His body was hard and thick and melded perfectly to hers, and she wanted to feel so much more. Marion brought her hands to his shoulders and pulled at them. He groaned in his throat and slid one hand down to cup her bottom which was near impossible to find considering the layers of her skirt. After shifting his hand a couple of different ways, the action struck her as humorous as laughter welled up from within her.

Probably from the nervous excitement of their shared passion, but in the next moment, Marion had released him and was laughing as she tried to catch her breath. His bewildered expression made her humor all the more ridiculous, yet it was unrelenting.

"Lady Marion, you must tell me what amuses you," he said, clearly not sharing her mirth.

"I do apologize, my lord. But you see, my gown—well, my gown has many parts to it." Her mirth turned to embarrassment, for how could she tell him he'd been nowhere near his intended mark.

Realization dawned on him and thankfully, he was not too arrogant to realize the relative impossibility of him ever finding her buttocks.

"I see, my lady. Your mirth is about the situation rather than my attempt."

"Aye, my lord, for I much enjoy your attempts," she said, wondering where this wanton response came from. That wasn't true; she knew exactly from where. From the same place that throbbed and pulsed every time he laid hands and lips on her. And she was growing to enjoy it.

"Well then, next time," he said leaning close to her ear so that his hot breath spread down her neck, "I shall find alternative access."

He then straightened and offered his arm again as if nothing had happened.

"Now come, my lady. I need to finish this discussion with you before we have need of an entirely different one."

THEY SAT ON a stone bench overlooking the loch for a spell so that Alexander could collect his thoughts. What was happening to him? He'd always held confidence when in the presence of a woman, even one for whom he'd held a passionate interest. But this? Nay, this was territory for which he had no navigation.

His plan was sound. Under a formal courtship, they could spend time together and really see if they were compatible in more than just a physical way. His first betrothal had been arranged by his father and, well, he was not prepared to venture down that path at the moment.

"My lord, you wished to ask me something?"

He turned to her and attempted a smile. "Aye. Lady Marion, will you allow me to court you?"

Her brow knit for a moment. "Court me, my lord? Is that not a question for my father?"

"Aye, I do wish to speak with your father, but in the meantime, will you accept that the king has given his blessing?"

Marion opened and closed her mouth a couple of times as if she did not know what her response would be. This was not how

Alexander hoped the conversation would go.

She drew in a deep breath and stood a little straighter. "And will you send word to my father?"

"Aye, I will send word immediately if you agree." He waited for what felt like an eternity. "Do you agree, Lady Marion? Will you let me court you so that I may know you better?"

Thankfully his last comment brought a wee smile to her lips. "Aye, my lord, I will let you court me."

"Excellent," he said. "I assure you I offer you the highest level of respect, and from this moment on, you shall have a chaperone with you at all times to protect your reputation. The king has planned to remain here for some days, and I do hope that is your plan as well?"

"Aye, I understand I am to remain here during their stay and return to Linlithgow with them at the end of their tour."

"Then it is all set. I will return you to the ladies and begin my planning. There is so much I wish to show you, Lady Marion," he said genuinely, meaning that in the best possible way. From now until she returned to Linlithgow, he would not lay a finger on her. He would allow nothing to jeopardize her reputation.

As they returned to the castle, he noted she seemed a little quiet, but he didn't have time to inquire for his mind was abuzz with ideas on how to entertain her. He found the other ladies and then kissed Marion's hand and headed off to see his steward. All who witnessed the gesture would be left in no doubt of its meaning. The thought of sharing all that he loved in his realm with her brought a sense of contentment he had not felt in a very long time. He would cover every inch of the grounds with her and every part of their lands. He was proud of his family and the effort they had put into making the castle and the grounds a haven.

It was clear to him that she had an interest in his manuscripts and particularly the ones containing the local legends and he knew exactly how to best present them to her.

After giving instructions to his steward and his sister, Alexander spent the remainder of the afternoon tracking down Gordon, who was one of the elder crofters who knew these woods and hills better than anyone.

"You're a hard man to track down."

The elder man whose beard had grown to almost his waist didn't look up from his whittling and merely replied, "A clever man is only found when he wants to be." Then with a grin, he added, "What can I do for you, wee lad?"

The endearment was always welcome to Alexander's ears. For he'd known Gordon all his life and considered him with the highest respect. The first time the man called him my lord after his elevation in status, Alexander corrected him, and the topic was never broached again.

"I have made some new friends," he said.

"Aye, aye, I have heard about the hustle and bustle at the castle. Och, sure you've the king himself down there these days."

"Aye, I do, and they have an interest in the old monk's tales."

This perked Gordon's attention fully then. He met Alexander's gaze and grinned. "And that they should. Those are our stories, and they should be told properly."

"I was thinking the exact same thing," he said. "So ye will come by after dark and tell them proper, then?"

"Aye, aye," he said and went back to his whittling. "Will there be ale?"

"There will be ale."

"Then I'll see ye after dark, wee lad."

Alexander's heart lifted as he left the man to his task. Gordon was a well-loved fixture in the village near Inverary Castle and Alexander could not imagine a better person to paint a picture of what their lives were like in the west Highlands. Surely Marion would find life here different than in the lowlands, but he was determined to share everything he loved about his home with her and hopefully she would feel the same way.

He took his time making his way back to the castle and thought about how close they had become in so short a time.

They seemed to possess a like-minded way of thinking and maybe that was why they had connected so quickly. But the passion that arose in him was surprising coming from an innocent. It was as though she'd had training or some such thing. Though he knew that to be impossible, it was difficult for him to push those thoughts away entirely. She'd ensnarled him completely and that had never happened to him before. So, what was it about her that pulled him into her graces? He would need a tremendous amount of willpower to keep her at arm's length and his hands off her until such time as they were to become married. As much as he wanted her—and oh, aye, he wanted her—he would do nothing to taint her reputation as he had already taken liberties he had no business taking.

As he approached the stable, his brother Thomas was waiting for him.

"All well there, brother?"

Thomas looked concerned, but then he always had something devastating on his mind.

"All is as well as it can be."

"Och, what does that mean?"

"Everyone saw you kiss that lady's hand. So, are ye betrothed now? Will ye toss her aside like ye did poor Eileen?"

Alexander was sick to his back teeth of Thomas's judgment in the matter of Eileen and in any matter where he didn't agree with decisions that had been made without his consult.

"Lady Marion and I are courting at this moment in time, Thomas, not that I need explain myself to you."

"I was just asking, brother. The rest of us have to bear the brunt of your mistakes."

"Really," Alexander said as he stopped to square off with Thomas. He wasn't in the mood for this juvenile behavior in one who should more than know how to behave like a man. "And exactly how have you been harmed by decisions that I have made?"

Alexander was a good four inches taller than Thomas and had

rarely stood this closely to him so as to emphasize the fact, but today and while they had guests, he'd put him in his place.

"I just mean, brother," Thomas said as he stepped back, "that after you discarded Eileen, some of the staff and villagers commented to me that they thought it was cruel of you."

"And why did they or you withhold this information until now? Why would you bring up a circumstance you do not understand which occurred nearly two years ago, now when I am considering a decision that only affects my future happiness? Really, Thomas, you have always been a maker of trouble, and I am here to tell you to drop this."

"Or what? What will you do if I reveal your true nature to your new lady? Does she know that after Eileen was forced to marry that man that she took her own life?"

Alexander grabbed Thomas by the scruff of his neck then and shook him. "Now you listen to me. If you cannot find it in your trouble making mind to stay out of my business, I will have you removed from this place permanently, and you know I can do it."

"I would like to see you try," he said and pulled out of Alexander's grasp. "Jean would never let you send me away."

Alexander leaned in close to Thomas and said in a low, menacing voice, "She will not know until it is done. You will cease this mischief and act like the gentleman you are supposed to be, or you will be banished."

With that, Thomas stalked away. Alexander was at his wit's end with the young man who acted more and more like a spoiled child every day.

The rustle of a skirt caught his attention, and he stepped forward a few paces to find his sister pretending to check the roses in the hedge.

"I am sorry you had to witness that, sister," he said.

"I witnessed nothing, brother," she said as she turned to him. "I was coming to find you to see if you had found Gordon and if he would join us this evening."

Jean was ever the peacemaker in the family and had an uncanny ability to know when to make a point and when to move on from it. By offering no comment, she was agreeing with Alexander and clearly had no intention of concurring with Thomas's assessment, nor would she stir Alexander's ire any further. A true politician.

"Aye, and in his own way, I believe he is excited at the prospect of telling our stories."

"You mean you got a sideways half smile?" she asked, now wearing a broad one herself.

"I did. And I am certain I know which story he will embellish the most."

"Aye, Glaistig is his favorite by far. How many times has she tried to drown him now?"

"At least nine or ten by now," Alexander said as he put his arm around his sister and walked with her inside the castle and onward to the great hall.

"But truly, sister, you do trust me, do you not?"

"Aye, Alexander. I trust you. We all do. Now you have to go and find something nice to wear for dinner and a visit from our Gordon. And maybe a wash," she said and took a large step away from him. "Ye smell like yer horse."

As she made the last comment, she ducked out of the great hall with her laughter following her to whomever she was set off to torment next.

He took a moment to admire the work she'd put into arranging the hall so that after their evening meal, the tables could be easily pushed back to enjoy a country dance if they wished it, and then the highlight which would be the telling of tales. Gordon would begin and would likely tell more than one, and after that it was custom for some of the staff to join in telling their own tall tales which sometimes included a jest or two at the laird's expense, but he didn't mind that as his staff were well cared for, and their respect was mutual.

Aye, it would be a grand evening, and he was very much looking forward to showing the king that a full and enjoyable time did not require lavishness and spectacle. Good food and good company were all that was required to achieve perfect contentment. He sincerely hoped that Marion shared his vision.

CHAPTER TWELVE

MARION COULD NOT have been more confused in the complete and utter change in Alexander the moment she agreed to let him court her. Not that she wanted her reputation sullied, but he grew almost cold to her in that moment. Did he have a different idea of what courtship meant? She shook her head as she pulled her brush through her hair. His sister had just come to say that they would be meeting in the great hall for their evening meal soon and she was to join them once she was dressed.

Marion had waved off the servant girl who was sent to aid her since the gown she'd chosen for this evening was far simpler than the ones she'd worn at Linlithgow. This was one of her own choosing which was dark green velvet with a square neckline and gold embroidery all across the edging and front of the bodice. 'Twas certainly not of the fashion worn by the ladies of the palace gatherings, but she was more comfortable in this one than any of theirs.

Finishing her hair off with a fine gold wreath, she left her chamber and made her way down the long stone hallway and toward the winding stairs that led to the front of the castle. Inverary was beautifully decorated with so many tapestries depicting battles or scenes of Loch Fyne or even of the surrounding woods in the fall when the colors exploded. She longed to see that particular natural spectacle in person. But as they would only remain here for a couple of days, she wondered what would happen once she returned to Posso Tower. He'd not spoken of a timeframe for the courtship, and as such, she was not sure entirely what to expect. Would he spend time with her and then forget her once she left? Marion had no idea.

Under normal circumstances, her father would have been in conversation with the earl and arranged terms and future intent. She was not equipped to ask such questions, and she did not think it appropriate to have to. Rather, he should have offered that information considering her inexperience. The more she thought about it, the more irritated she became. But that would not do as she was a guest here and she'd fast become friends with Lady Jean as well as continuing her friendship with the queen. Nay, she would not let the confounding actions of a man ruin her ability to enjoy a wonderful meal and evening in a place for which she grew a fond affection.

Marion squared her shoulders and lifted her chin as she entered the great hall to find Lady Jean, some of her younger brothers, and the earl all seated by the fire laughing at something the youngest was saying. The moment Alexander caught sight of her, he was on his feet and striding toward her. By God, he was intense. It was absolutely impossible to tear her gaze from him when he pinned her so.

"Good evening, Lady Marion. You are truly a sight to behold this evening," he said as he reached for her hand to kiss it. For a moment he merely gazed at her and stroked the back of her hand with his thumb. She caught the fresh scent of him with notes of lavender and leather and wanted to lean in and bury her face in his shirt to inhale deeply.

His lips parted and she stared as he swallowed and drew in a shaky breath. "My lady, you cannot look at me like that," he whispered.

Mortified, she met his gaze and realized he must have some sort of magic in him to have so clearly read her thoughts. She pulled her hand out of his grasp and stepped back.

Alexander stood a little taller and offered her his arm with his previously passion-filled gaze fully masked.

"Shall we sit while we await our meal?"

"Aye," she said and walked past him to take a seat next to Jean, leaving him to sit across from her rather than beside her.

After a moment or two, he stood and moved to stand by the hearth with his arm rested over his head along the stone decoration. He stared into the fire, leaving her to turn her attention to Jean.

"I understand there is to be storytelling here this evening," she said.

"Aye, my lady, we have the best storytellers in all of Scotland, to be sure."

"That's true, Lady Marion," the littlest brother Archibald said.

"And what are your favorite stories about, Archibald is it?"

"Everyone calls me Archie, so you can call me Archie."

"Very well, Archie, what are your favorite stories about?"

"I cannae tell ye, my lady."

"Oh really," she said, surprised at his conviction. "And why is that?"

"Because we cannae start until Gordon tells his first and then we can join in."

Marion was not sure what that meant, but it was important to little Archie so she would not press him. "Very well, then, Archie. I believe I very much look forward to hearing your story."

From the corner of her eye, she became aware of Alexander's gaze on her. His hot and cold manners were becoming exhausting. She turned her attention back to Jean.

"We do something similar in my home after an evening meal, but we tell our stories through music. Sometimes one of us will add our voices to the pipes and strings, but other times I have found I can lose myself in the beautiful notes."

"I can only imagine how lovely that is. My brother tells me you hail from Stobo."

"Aye, we do not have a castle as lavish as this, but 'tis a tower house very near that village."

"Do you have to climb up the tower on a ladder?" Archie asked.

Marion enjoyed his curiosity. "Nay, wee man, we have winding stairs that if you run up them too fast, will make you dizzy and you could fall all the way to the bottom. I can still hear my mother yelling at me and my sister, 'no running on those stairs lest ye break yer heads,' but we didn't listen to her."

Archie laughed and came alongside Marion to touch her hair. She loved how honest innocent little children could be. Her red hair was very different than the dark hair that ran through this family, and it was clear he liked it.

"Did a witch turn you into a vampire?"

Marion laughed. She'd heard this legend before. "Well now, wee man, maybe I will have to wait and tell that story later."

For a moment his eyes went wide, and he dropped the lock of her hair he'd been holding.

"But I think this Gordon will forgive us if we tell this one early, aye?"

Eyes still wide, Archie merely nodded.

"My mother told me that when I was a wee lass, my hair was blonde. One day I was walking through the flowers in the meadow, and I fell asleep on a bed of orange hawkweed. I slept for hours as my mother called and called for me. When she found me and I woke up, my hair was red and has been red ever since."

Little Archie's eyes were large as saucers and his mouth was agape as he listened to her.

"Is that true?" Archie's sister, Cora, asked, now taking great interest in Marion and her hair.

"Well, I mean, 'tis what my mother told me, so it has to be true, right?"

Archie turned to Alexander then. "Alex, is that true? Did Lady Marion's hair turn red from the orange weeds?"

Alexander gave Marion a broad smile which told her he approved of her not feeding into Archie's obvious scary imagination.

"I have heard that if you fall asleep in a bed of bluebells, your hair will turn blue, so I do believe it is a true tale. And I do not believe Lady Marion capable of telling tall ones like some boys I know."

Marion noted a few things in that last exchange. That Alexander allowed his younger siblings to shorten his given name was as endearing as anything she'd seen in this family thus far. Secondly, that he so quickly jumped in to support her attempt at a story was a side of him she hadn't realized she wanted. Her mind turned over and over with what she truly wanted from him and the conclusion was she did not know.

"I do not tell tall tales," he said and folded his little arms across his chest.

"You do," Cora said. "You fib all the time."

"I do not."

"Now, now," Jean said and separated them as they had been clearly about to get into a scrap. "Keith, take Archie outside until the meal is served. Cora, you come sit with me and practice your ladylike manners."

Marion's heart was warmed. She missed her siblings and was comforted by the genuine interaction of this family. And there it was. The unmistakable knowledge that a certain older brother's gaze was yet again fixed on her.

ALEXANDER EXCUSED HIMSELF from his sister and Marion to see to Keith and Archie once the servants entered one by one to set up for the meal. In truth, he needed a break from the war raging within him. He was having a harder time by the moment being in her presence and having to refrain from taking her in his arms and begging her to kiss him. No gown she'd worn up to that moment could compare to the one she donned this evening, which to him encapsulated her natural aura. And the care with which she engaged with his siblings made him want her even more. She possessed a kind soul and a quick wit. How in heaven would he be able to resist her until he could speak with her father? By God, he would have to plunge in the cold loch twice a day to keep himself in check.

He found his brothers and together they returned to the great hall. By now the servants had fully adorned the table with large floral arrangements from the gardens as well and brought up platters of roasted deer, wild boar, smoked mackerel, and the usual mounds of breads and cheese. The king had offered the queen's special mead recipe ahead of time so the brewers could have some on hand for this visit.

The king and queen were also now in attendance and had taken their seats, the king of course at the head of the table and the queen to his left. Alexander sat across from her with Jean beside him and then Thomas and down the line with his siblings. Marion sat next to the queen and across from Jean. He was pleased that he could address the queen but also see Marion without looking directly at her, for he could not stand the king's jest at him drooling over her like an unsullied lad.

"Did you enjoy the tour of our grounds today, Your Majesty?" he asked the queen.

"Yes, I did very much so, my lord. Your gardeners are true magicians in how they have incorporated the natural beauty into sculpted artistry. One does not always need the exotic to find true beauty."

Alexander couldn't agree more. He'd been thinking much the same about Marion. While other ladies clamored to impress the queen and adopt her styles, Marion was much more comfortable with her own and true Scottish style, and he admired that. He allowed his gaze to flick to her and offer a small smile.

"I understand there is to be entertainment this eve," the king said.

"Aye, my lord, although I am afraid none can compare to that which you offer at Linlithgow and Stirling."

The king nodded in agreement. It was obvious to anyone paying attention that he wanted that to be the opinion not only in all of Scotland and Britain, but in all of Europe as well.

"You should see what I have planned for Stirling next year," he said as he squeezed his wife's hand.

Next year, the young queen would come of age, and it was widely rumored that the king had a coming out party planned the like the Continent had never seen.

"I anticipate it will be one for the written histories," he said.

"Indeed," the king said. "Indeed, it will."

The conversation was light for the remainder of the meal. Alexander paid as much attention to Marion as was appropriate, but in his mind, he recalled every detail of their encounters together: the way she smelled, how soft she was in his arms, the taste of her lips, and the look in her eyes when her passions heightened. God, he was sure it had suddenly become warm in the hall as his trews tightened around his loins.

"Argyll, something troubles you?" the king asked.

Turning to him and surprised anyone had noticed him, he said, "I am well, my lord. Maybe a wee full from the meal and the ale."

As if on perfect cue, the servants filled the hall and waited for the signal to move the tables and food to set up for the evening's entertainment. Alexander excused himself and stepped outside to catch a breath of fresh air. Again, he asked himself how he could conceal his true feelings for Marion for modesty's sake and her reputation. Guests be damned, he wanted to march back in there and hoist her over his shoulder then carry her off to a night of endless pleasuring. If the way she responded to his kisses was any indication, he would have her writhing beneath him and begging for release. And she would have it. As many times as she desired.

He had to get a hold of himself lest he make a complete and utter ass of himself and embarrass her.

"Ahh, there you are," his sister said. "Everyone is waiting for you to start," she said and then ducked her head to take in his expression. "Brother, are you unwell or are you just unable to take your mind off that ethereal creature you are courting?"

"Be kind, Jean," he said. He was in no mood for her jesting.

"As I see it, you have to choose between acting like a gentleman versus a randy schoolboy or marrying the lass. I see no other alternative for you, but I will say this much. She does not know you like I do, and I believe she is interpreting your frustrations with yourself as dissatisfaction with her. So, fix that. Now."

With that she walked away, leaving him with more questions than answers. In any case, there would be none of them this night. Alexander straightened himself and returned to the great hall. The tables and chairs had been arranged so that all focus would be on a sole chair just in front of the hearth.

The king and queen were, of course, in the center with a chair left for Alexander and Marion seated beside him. It was just as well. He needed to be able to sit beside her and keep his hands to himself. And he would be sure she understood that his internal struggles were his and were not a reflection or any fault of hers.

"Has Gordon been shown in?" he asked his sister just before she took her seat.

"Aye, he is here and well primed," she said with a grin.

Gordon was the only man Alexander had ever known who could drink his weight in ale and never show it. The only tell was that he stood a little taller and spoke a little clearer.

Sitting next to Marion with the firelight on her features, Alexander could not recall another time he'd been preoccupied with his own future, family, children, the future of the clan. All of it ran through his mind in a flash the moment he caught her gaze.

"I am glad you are seated next to me, Lady Marion. I do hope that you enjoy our version of telling stories, though I look forward to experiencing yours as well."

"Aye, my lord, I am very much looking forward to this as I have always discovered that during such tellings, various truths are gleaned that may help us understand one another better."

He couldn't agree more and once again admired the way her mind turned.

"You will find that is very much the case with us as well, but I must warn you," he said and leaned in close to her ear, "some of Gordon's tales should be taken with a grain of salt."

She laughed which was a delight to his ears. The thought of his actions and struggles causing her discomfort did not sit well with him. He would be sure to be far more mindful in the future with her.

"I assumed as much, my lord. Though I admit, 'tis wee Archie's stories I am most interested in hearing."

"Now those are tall, despite the wee lad's height."

"May I ask you something?"

"Aye, please do, my lady."

"I noticed your younger siblings calling you by a shortened version of your given name."

"Aye."

"Is that a tradition in your family?"

"Aye, I suppose it is. My father always encouraged us to do that versus my lord which he felt was far too formal. We keep the formality with the staff and villagers so as to maintain distinction, but even Gordon there calls me wee man just the same as he did when I was but a bairn."

"I like that. My family are quite informal with one another as well. Thank you for being open and honest with me."

He nodded and then sat back, pleased as Gordon commanded the attention of everyone in the hall.

CHAPTER THIRTEEN

T HE MAN INTRODUCED himself as Gordon, and from that moment, Marion hung off every word that fell from his lips. The chair was there for him to sit and sometimes he did, but mostly he moved about the crowd weaving his tales of faeries and sprites, of witches and selkies, and she loved every second of it.

"But the worst of 'em is a creature so cunning ye don't know you're under her spell until 'tis too late." He sat for this story and seemed to enjoy the gasps among the crowd. "Glaistig is what the old folk called her. Nine times she's tried to drown me in the loch, but I outwit her every time, that I do.

"Now, you mind when walking these woods if ye see a stream, ye better turn the other way, for there she will be waiting all dressed in green with a long skirt to hide her goat legs. She will call your name sweetly and ask ye for aid, but don't turn toward her for that's when she will cast her spell and draw you to the water.

"She's nearly gotten me, but I know her ways now. I know how to ward her off."

Marion leaned forward, for though the stories of myths and legends were abundant in her neck of the woods, she'd never heard anything like this Glaistig which seemed far more malevolent than a ghostly piper or a will-o'-the-wisp.

"And do ye want to know how, lass?"

So taken with his story was she that she jumped slightly when he addressed her directly. She nodded, not trusting her voice.

"Aye, well ye see, ye have to call her by her real name. I heard her singing it to herself one day and that's how I knew."

Marion cleared her voice and dared ask, "And what is her name?"

"I dare not say it out loud, lest we might summon her. But I'll whisper it to ye," he said and motioned her forward.

Marion looked up at Alexander who nodded to her. Standing on shaky legs, she approached the old man and leaned close to his ear.

"BOO!"

Marion jumped and squealed then burst into laughter as she realized his jest. Delighted with him, she kissed his cheek and then took her seat again. Others around her laughed and clapped and she joined in what then became a standing round of applause for him.

He graciously bowed then invited anyone else to share their tales. She turned to Alexander and caught his broad grin which resulted in a little flip-flop in her belly. By God, but he was handsome, and she couldn't recall a time when she so thoroughly enjoyed herself.

"Your man is very talented," she said to him.

"Aye, he is a treasure to be sure. And he never tells the same story in the same way."

Marion could believe it. The twinkle in his eyes told her plenty of the mischief that lay behind them. She'd never met anyone who possessed that kind of charisma.

Next up was little Archie, and Marion found herself leaning forward again while the lad prepared himself, clearly loving the attention that was already befalling him.

Alexander cleared his throat to quiet those around them and then nodded at Archie. "Go ahead, lad," he said quietly.

Archie pulled himself up to his full height and Marion was surprised when he spoke in a loud clear voice.

"My name is Archie, and I am here to tell of a tale that is even scarier than Gordon's Glaistig. My story begins deep in the loch when the moon is high and bright. On those nights when you are all tucked and snug in your bed, ye may want to pull them up a little higher for out of the loch flies Fanny Wi' Four Teeth, and if ye look in her eyes she will steal ye away to the loch to keep for ever and ever."

Overly exaggerated gasps could be heard all around, making Marion smile.

"Have ye ever seen her?" someone asked from the crowd.

"Aye," he said and stood up and paced like Gordon had. "I saw her one night through granny's old, knitted blanket. I saw her but she never saw me and then she flew away again."

"Tell us another!"

The look of pride on Archie's face in that moment made Marion's heart swell. She stole a glance at Alexander and could see water welling in his eyes. Without thinking, she placed her hand on his arm and squeezed. He blinked a few times then smiled down at her.

"He's a natural," she said.

"Aye, that he is, and I believe maybe spending too much time with Gordon."

"You have a lovely family, my lord," she said.

"I am glad you approve," he said and placed his large hand over hers. "And if we are courting, you must call me by my given name when we are speaking alone. I believe I may enjoy hearing it from your lips."

Marion's breath caught in her throat. She searched his expression for jest, but there was none.

"And I would like to hear my name on yours as well," she said, not meaning for her voice to have taken a deep tone.

Alexander sucked in his breath and let it hiss through his teeth. "You are making it very difficult for me to keep my vow," he said, his voice low and deep.

"And what vow is that, Alexander?" she asked.

"My vow to ensure your reputation is intact during our courtship. I vowed I would not lay a hand on you, but that is increasingly impossible when you look at me the way you do."

She didn't know in what way he meant; she just knew that she couldn't stop looking at him and couldn't stop thinking of how delicious she felt when he kissed her.

"And why would you vow such a thing without telling me?" she asked, now realizing where the hot and cold came from.

"I—I suppose I was protecting your virtue."

"I believe I may have a say in my virtue as well, do I not?"

"Aye."

"Then, my lord Alexander, please do not refrain from kissing me anytime we are alone."

"You do not mean that surely," his voice barely above a whisper now.

Marion did mean it as in her mind if they were courting, they were testing their compatibility and that included kissing. There she let the thought complete itself in her mind.

"I do mean it."

"And what if I want more than kissing?"

"For that you shall have to wait."

"Marion, every time I kiss you, I want more."

She was pleased for his honesty, but it took a great deal of courage to reveal her own truths with him. Still, the constant guessing what his feelings were was exhausting.

"Very well, we shall keep the kissing to a minimum, but there will be some. That is my requirement in this courtship. And you will not hide your feelings for me, nor I from you."

He took far too many heartbeats to reply, but a slow smile spread across his firm lips. She found herself looking at them and was again distracted by the memory of how they felt pressed against hers.

"Lady Marion, you drive a hard bargain. I accept your terms," he said and reached out his hand.

They shook hands and then he kissed the back of hers. "I do

not believe even the most difficult of the king's tests of skill have challenged me as much as this arrangement with you."

Marion laughed. "Surely you jest, my lord—"

"Alexander."

"Alexander, surely you jest. For I have seen you atop your horse barreling toward your next opponent. That, sir, takes great skill."

"Aye, it does indeed. But the constant need to restrain myself from carrying you off to the nearest bed so I can bury myself inside you until we are both depleted of our strength is much, much harder."

His lips were so close to hers, all she had to do was lean forward and the entire hall would be privy to a scandal that could only end one way.

The din in the hall broke through then, and she sat back regarding his expression. His eyes were dark like a stormy sea, and he looked like he could devour her. When their time came, and she knew in that moment that it would, she wondered if she would survive it.

She did have some idea of what happened between a man and a woman, but even her limited interactions with him were far more than she could have even imagined. What more did she have to learn?

Alexander gave her one final longing look and then turned back to the next storyteller, making himself ready to please a demanding crowd. Marion drew in a deep breath and prayed no one else in the hall had caught the intensity that had just passed between them.

WHY ON EARTH he had agreed to such terms he could not say. But he was certain that if he did not restrain his growing passion for her, there would be no need to wait for her to return to Linlithgow for her parents' blessing. He would marry her on the morrow and ease his ever-tightening loins by tomorrow eve. God, that thought didn't help his burden. Merely sitting next to her was becoming torture, and to hear her demand kissing her was about all he could take. How on earth could a maiden and a lady say such things without knowing about lovemaking? Damned if he knew, but he was determined to keep her chaste until such time as they were wed.

The last thought surprised him. He thought his plan was sound. He could court her and then formalize a betrothal and marry sometime in the new year. At this rate, at least a betrothal was out the window. And was it fair to rush this with her just because he needed to be inside her? Had he actually said that? But she hadn't recoiled from the comment either, so what did that mean? She either knew what he meant and wanted it, or she had no idea what he was talking about. His mind went round in circles.

He would have to confess, he did not pay much attention to the remaining stories that thankfully went well into the eve so that even the queen and king wished to retire rather than turn the evening into a late-night ceilidh. They'd save that for another night. He was sure the king had been somewhat amused, but had not displayed his normal joviality that was visible at his own gatherings.

Once all the guests retreated from the hall and only Marion and Alexander remained, save for a few servants, he turned to her.

"Shall I escort you to your chamber, my lady?"

"Aye, my lord, I believe that would be acceptable."

All formal in front of the servants, but he had every intention of tasting her sweet lips before heading off to his slumber.

Up the winding staircase they walked together and down the long hallway to her chamber. He'd given up his rooms and Jean had given up hers for their majesties, so he was down another hall and on the opposite side of the castle from Marion. Which was a good thing.

Once at her door, she turned to him and peeked around to see if anyone was about. She then reached up on tip toes and kissed him sweetly on the lips.

"See, that wasn't so painful now, was it?"

Even something so brief very much was.

"No, my lady Marion, that was not painful," he said and leaned down to cup her face in his hands. He brushed his lips across hers and slowly parted her lips with his before claiming her mouth. She tasted of berries and sunshine and his mind raced with images of them making love in a meadow with a clear blue sky overhead.

Before he would let himself become too deep into the kiss, he ended it. A necessary move to keep himself from kicking open her door and flinging her on the bed, but also to show her just how dangerous a game she played.

"Did that kiss satisfy the terms of our agreement?" he asked.

She stepped away and smoothed her hair and then her skirts.

"Aye, my lord, I believe that shall satisfy our agreement quite nicely. Every time we are alone. We agreed."

Alexander drew a deep breath and smiled. "You also agreed to use my given name," he said as he drew her forward with his hands on her waist and kissed her sweetly and softly again. "Let me hear it, Marion. Let me hear you say my name."

"Alexander," she whispered.

This time he claimed her lips fast and hard as he pushed her up against the stone wall and pressed his body hard into hers. A second later, he released her and stared hard into her eyes.

"Good night, Marion," he said and did not wait for a reply.

Striding to his bed chamber, he raked his hands through his hair. He prayed there was a basin of cold water waiting for him so that he could splash some on his face.

He was not disappointed. A large basin of cool water along with a tankard of ale and a goblet rested on a table beside the fire. Thankfully it was not as raging as his erection.

By God, but that woman set him ablaze. And it was not just sexual. He was drawn in by her wit, her compassion, her kindness, and her strength of character. Truly the woman was like she was made for him.

But that was what she was groomed to be, was it not? He tried to push away those intrusive thoughts that made him doubt her sincerity when she had given him absolutely no reason. Just because others had less honorable intentions, didn't mean she did. It was going to be a very long night if he couldn't turn off these mistrusting ideas. She was perfect in every way possible, and despite her parents' interest in an advantageous match, there was no indication that was her design. Was there?

Dammit.

Alexander undid his belt and shrugged out of his tunic and shirt. Splashing water on his face and chest helped a little, but not enough. He poured a goblet of ale and downed it then poured another.

As he sat by the hearth, he thought about how kind she'd been to little Archie earlier and how unembarrassed she'd been when falling for Gordon's jest. Nay, no one was that much of an actor. He could come to no other conclusion than that she was as perfect as she appeared to be.

In that case, then why would there be a need for a delay? He'd send a rider to her parents on the morrow informing them they would be wed at Inverary and would then travel to Linlithgow.

The king would be delighted and there would be cause for yet another feast at the palace. This time, Marion's parents would be the guests of honor and all would be happy.

Right.

He supposed he should ask her first. Smiling, he thought of how she would react if he returned to her chamber this evening and posed the question to her then and there, and he had to confess to himself he could not recall a time when his body welled with excitement.

His father had spoken to him of arrangements for his future and he'd long refused, insisting he wanted to be sure of his match when the time was right. And now he certainly was. Jean was already of marrying age and Thomas needed a purpose. With Marion around, the younger siblings would have a female influence and that would free Jean up to find her own future and Thomas…well, Thomas would need to start thinking about his future too.

It all seemed perfect. Too perfect—and there went his mistrusting thoughts again.

Alexander stripped off his trews and crawled into bed. He tossed and turned for what felt like hours before finally slipping into a restless slumber. All night he envisioned Marion and him living and thriving at Inverary, raising children of their own when he finally sat bolt upright somewhere around the crack of dawn.

What if she didn't want to live at Inverary? What if she preferred Posso Tower or worse, Linlithgow!

He couldn't take it any longer and so threw on his clothes again and splashed more water on his face then left his chamber to head to the stables.

Once there, he drew his horse from the stall and prepared him for a quiet morning ride. This time of day with the foggy dew rolling across the loch was his favorite, for here in these moments before the world awoke, he could find solace. As he drew from the stable, he caught sight of a long cloak moving toward the other side of the gardens. Curious, he secured his horse in the stall and made his way to follow.

Alexander meandered through the garden until he heard a female giggle and a deep man's voice return the sentiment.

He'd stumbled upon a couple engaged in a tryst and was now obligated to discover them. He followed the sound until he was sure the couple were around the next corner. Damn the designer of this maze.

"Who goes there?" a man's voice called.

"Laird of this place," he said as he turned the corner to discover the couple. His heart skipped a beat as he found his sister Jean in the arms of his best friend and steward Alain.

Alexander had no words for the shock of the scene. Still in one another's embrace, the look of mortification on Jean's face was immeasurable.

"Brother, I can explain," she said.

"Well, someone had better," he said. "Because I am about to draw swords."

His mind buzzed. Were they new lovers or had this been going on for some time? Was there sex involved or had he discovered them in time?

All thoughts of his own plans flew away with the morning mist as he watched them disentangle.

"I can explain, my lord," Alain said.

"You will return to your home and await me there." To Jean, he said, "You will await me in the library. Go straight there and say nothing to anyone. Do you understand me?"

"Aye, brother," she said, and he was certain he'd caught sight of tears in her eyes as he passed.

Alexander did not wait to hear what Alain had to say for himself. He could not hear the man's words at the moment. What he might have said if the man had come and spoken to him, he did not know. But this was betrayal beyond acceptance.

CHAPTER FOURTEEN

MARION STRETCHED AND rolled over to gaze out at the pinkish-gray morning sky. She'd passed a fitful night, but in truth she was not troubled. She was, in fact, a little proud of herself for expressing what she wanted and was pleased that he was not so arrogant as to deny her some form of control over their relationship. Because they were in one now, whether either of them was ready for it or not.

Her thoughts drifted to the way he commanded her body when he pressed her against the wall. Thrilling shivers raced through her at the memory. Marion turned over onto her back and flicked her arm above her head. By God, but he was like something out of a dream. Everything about him drew her in and held her breathless under his spell. Maybe he was a magical creature straight out of one of the stories told last eve.

She smiled as she threw back the covers and got out of bed. It was too early to expect servants and so she donned a robe and stepped over to the window to gaze out over the beautiful gardens at the back of the castle. When she did, she caught sight of something unexpected.

Jean hurried away from the gardens with Alexander tight on her heels; behind them and, dragging his feet, was a very forlorn-looking Alain. What on earth could have passed that would cause so much distress among them?

She rummaged until she found her shift and a plain gown she'd brought for daily wear then dragged her brush through her hair. She quietly exited her chamber after she was dressed and made her way downstairs. Just as she took the last step, Alexander and Jean entered the library and closed the door.

Not knowing if she would be unwelcome, she hesitated and walked toward the outside to see where the other man had gone. She found him pacing just outside the castle.

"Is aught amiss?" she asked, not knowing what else to say.

"Lady Marion, I am certain you mean well, but this matter is one of great delicacy as I am sure you can appreciate."

Then it all clicked into place. And she absolutely did not want to interfere with matters between a brother and sister.

"Very well, I shall leave you to your musings," she said and turned to retreat to her chamber.

Halfway back to the stairwell, the library door opened, and Alexander stepped out. His eyes widened at the sight of her, but then he frowned, and his brow drew in tight.

"Lady Marion, you are about early," he said. He was probing. That much was obvious.

"Aye, my lord, I rise early each morn."

"I shall have a servant attend you in your chamber."

"There is no need, my lord."

"Then why are you below stairs?"

She didn't like his tone. Did he think she was being nosy?

"I was gazing out of my chamber window at the beautiful gardens when I saw three people exit. I merely came below to see if I could offer assistance in some way."

"We have no need of your assistance, Lady Marion, and I trust I can rely on your discretion in this matter?"

It was clear from that comment, he didn't trust her judgment at all, and that did not sit well with her.

"Of course you can, my lord. I am surprised you even have to make such a comment."

"Lady Marion, if you do not require anything, I would ask

that you return to your chamber until the morning servants arrive to assist your morning routine. I will see you at the morning meal," he said and stalked off toward the great hall.

Marion stood there with her mouth agape. She had done nothing wrong, and while she could understand something upsetting had occurred, she did not think she should be discarded as such for attempting to help.

She was about to go after him and tell him so when the library door opened again, and a very teary-eyed Jean emerged. She looked startled when she realized she was not alone.

"Lady Jean, you are safe with me, I promise you."

"Where is my brother?"

"Well, after he ordered me to be discreet, he marched off to the great hall."

Jean's face was tear-streaked and she wrung her hands together hard while staring in the direction of the hall.

"I do not know what to do," she said.

Marion wrapped her arm around Jean's shoulder and squeezed.

"Is it really that bad?"

"Aye, you should have heard him. He is ready to banish me."

Shy of plotting his murder, what could she have possibly done to warrant that kind of reaction in him?

"Lady Marion, I asked you to return to your chamber," a booming voice said from behind her.

"I was about to when your sister emerged from the library. I assure you, my lord, I am not here to add to your strife."

"Then release my sister and do as I bid."

No one, not even her father, had ever spoken to her in such a way. Oh, she would go to her chamber all right and pack her belongings and leave this place before he could say morning meal.

Marion kissed Jean on the cheek and then lifted her chin to look Alexander square in the face. "I understand something has passed here that has upset you, and for that I am sorry. But I have done nothing except offer assistance which would have come with discretion. I shall return to my chamber and when I emerge again, I expect transportation arranged to return me to my parents."

With that, she turned on her heel and with squared shoulders, she ascended the stairs and made her way to her chamber. Once inside, she bolted it and then flung herself on her bed to let loose her emotions.

How could he possibly be so callous with her after all he'd declared the night before? She'd been understanding of the situation and his current state; he need not take his anger out on her nor insinuate she was not capable of discretion. Did that even need to be said? After what they'd shared. And now she only had mortification to accept at being so wanton with him and trusting that his feelings were as true as hers. Well, no more. She opened her clothes chest and quickly filled it with her belongings.

But now that she was ready to leave, she was not sure how. She'd eat her own tongue before she spoke another word to that odious man, but she would need him to arrange a carriage for her and have her chest brought down. And what about her dear friend Queen Margaret? How would she explain her need to be out of that man's sights without disclosing why?

Marion paced with one hand on her hip and another tapping her lips. Her heart raced as she realized she was in a predicament which she could not reason her way out of. Did she want to leave now? Aye, she very much did. But how could she leave without alerting others and drawing more attention to the situation?

She was trapped and she despised the panic rising within her. There was no way she could remain. She would have to find a way to get word to the queen. She glanced around the chamber and spied a quill, ink, and some parchment tucked behind a fat candleholder.

A few minutes later, she signed her brief note to the queen and folded it as neatly as she could. Maybe she could leave it for the servants to find.

A soft knock on the door interrupted her thoughts.

'My lady, it is Jean," a quiet voice spoke from the other side of the door.

Marion opened it and saw that both brother and sister were on the other side.

"What is it that you want?" she asked.

"We wish to apologize," she said.

"You have nothing to apologize for, Lady Jean. I have asked for transportation and assistance with my belongings. Has that been arranged?"

She did not dare look at Alexander, though she could feel his eyes upon her.

"Aye, my lady, but we do not want you to leave."

"It is too late for that now. I feel the need to be near my family and I wish to leave this place immediately," she said, still only meeting Jean's gaze. "I have left a note on the table there," she said and pointed to it. "Will you see to it that the queen receives it? Do not fret. I am merely apologizing to her for leaving abruptly and stated only that I have a sudden need to be with my family."

"Very well, then," Alexander said and turned on his heel to leave.

"I am so sorry," Jean said.

"Lady Jean, what happened?"

"I am in love, and my brother cannot handle the fact that he did not arrange it for me. I mean, I don't even think he's upset that it's Alain. I am not required to marry for title, and we are less formal than some families. I know Alex only wants me to be happy. But he is angry that he had to discover us by chance versus us having come to him directly, and so he feels we have betrayed him."

"I am very sorry, Lady Jean, and I truly hope he comes to terms with your choice. You deserve to be happy."

"But you are still leaving."

"I must. Your brother's behavior this morning was unacceptable, and I will not stay one moment longer here because of it."

Jean wrapped her arms around Marion and squeezed.

"My brother is in love with you, and he has no idea how to express himself. I hope someday you will be able to understand that."

Marion's only thought was that she needed to be out of this castle and as far away from Alexander Campbell as she could get.

ALEXANDER WRAPPED THE cloak over his head and sat next to the driver while the servants secured Marion's bags on the back of the carriage and she inside. He'd had the cook roused and prepare a basket of food and plenty of mead in a wine skin for her as well as blankets should she need them. She'd ride alone in the carriage, but he would not let her out of his sight. He'd already explained everything to the king who decided they would continue on their tour as well and was more than understanding of the situation. But at the same time, he appeared to find mirth in it for some reason. Alexander would never understand the man, but was grateful for his understanding and an open invitation to join them whenever he was in that part of the country.

Within a short time, they were off on the long journey to Linlithgow. He hoped the ride would help him clear his head about Jean and Alain. He'd left Thomas in charge of them and to ensure Alain did not come near the castle while Alexander was away.

By God, what a morning. And to think he'd had intention to send word to her parents today. Now he was delivering her to them. And then what? He honestly had no idea. Between the shock of Jean and Alain and the fact that she knew she had him twisted into knots, he knew not what he should do.

If he had to be honest with himself, he couldn't imagine a

better match for Jean than Alain, a man with whom he shared a strong bond. But why couldn't they have just told him for Christ's sake? Why did he have to discover them sneaking around like they were ashamed of it, or they feared his reaction?

And there it was. He'd proven to them he would react badly, hadn't he? On top of that, he'd taken his frustrations out on Marion who he could see now was merely trying to help. Oh aye, he was the worst arse this side of Loch Ness. By God, how badly he'd botched it all.

But he would fix it. One way or another, he'd make it right for all of them.

They rode for several hours until they came to a smallish village which housed a decent sized inn frequented by travelers from east to west and vice versa. Alexander stepped down from the carriage, his knees nearly buckling from the long ride. His driver, who had remained thankfully silent for the ride, waited for Alexander's next instruction.

The moment was now. He steadied himself for the coming storm.

Opening the door to the carriage at the same time he drew down the hood of his cloak, his eyes met hers. For a moment or two, she blinked at him and mouthed soundless words.

"We have arrived at an inn and will rest here for the evening, my lady. The journey is too long to achieve in one day."

She would obviously recall that from her journey there, but still she stared at him as though he were an apparition.

Reaching out his hand to her, he said, "My lady, will you join me for an evening meal? Neville will retrieve your chests and bring them to your chamber so that you may retire when you wish."

"How?" she asked, still appearing quite confused.

"I suspect he will untie the lashes and then pull them from the carriage and carry them," he said, attempting a jest to lighten the moment.

"Nay, I mean how did you get here?"

"I have been here the entire time. Do you really think I would let you travel across the country alone and without protection?"

And up came the chin once again. She really was becoming quite adept at silent defiance.

"I do not need your protection, my lord. I am perfectly capable of taking care of myself. And besides, the only one I need protecting from is you."

Och, that hurt. But he could appreciate its origins. She needed to tell him what was what, and he could not fault her for it. In fact, he'd welcome it as long as she was on speaking terms with him.

"I understand, my lady. In the meantime, there are several other large riders approaching, and I believe you might find it prudent to be inside and situated properly before that lot demands the best table."

The look of concern that crossed her face gave him just enough comfort that she now realized how dangerous traveling alone could be.

He reached out his hand again, and this time she took it and exited the carriage.

The moment her feet touched the ground, she withdrew her hand and walked on ahead of him.

Alexander could not help but grin at her stubbornness. She had every right to be vexed with him and he would take every shot she threw his way. He deserved it and he would be sure she was fully and completely free to speak her peace.

He ducked as he entered the inn, and his grin broadened when he spied her directing the innkeeper as to where she would like to sit. This was a place well known to him, and when the innkeeper spied him and made to leave her to dote on him, Alexander shook his head.

Once they were seated in the corner, she finally turned to him.

"You know you really hurt me this morn. There was no need of that."

"I know it and I am very sorry."

"Thank you. But I am still returning to my home."

"Aye, I know it and I understand."

"I trusted you. I thought we trusted one another. But the moment something went awry, you shut me out."

"Forgive me, Lady Marion. That is all I ask. I am unaccustomed to sharing responsibility when it comes to family matters."

"I believe we have very different views of what marriage is, my lord, and as such I am almost glad this instance has occurred to illustrate those differences."

"Lady Marion, you have made many incorrect assumptions this day and this latest is the largest of them. I feel we should not continue this conversation at this time as I would not wish things to be said that we cannot retract."

He could see by her pursed lips that she was none too pleased by his declaration. So much for letting her have her say. But she was going down a road that would lead to an impasse and he was not prepared to go there.

"If you do not oppose, my lord, I shall take my meal in my chamber and turn in early. I expect we shall be on our way at daybreak?"

If he could keep their driver out of his cups this evening they would, but he couldn't promise it.

"I will knock at your door when we are ready and will have a meal prepared for you to take while we journey."

"Very well, my lord. I bid you a fair eve."

With that she left the table, checked with the innkeeper, and went up the stairs to disappear around a corner to go to her chamber.

Alexander sat back in his chair and downed his goblet of ale. The barmaid brought him a steaming bowl of some sort of meat stew he was grateful for and devoured before asking for a second, along with a pitcher of ale. It would be a long night with thoughts of her crooked as sin stewing in her bed chamber and not working through this with him as he had hoped.

By God, she was stubborn.

The entire time they'd traveled that day, she had not tapped on the carriage once to ask to relieve herself. Not once, though they had stopped a few times to water the horses and for him and his rider to do the same. His driver had asked, but she'd refused. How does one go several hours in that state? He couldn't fathom. In any case, she was safe and secure in a locked chamber, of that he had secured, and he supposed he'd see how she fared after a good night's sleep.

Or so he hoped.

Chapter Fifteen

S HE AWOKE TO the sound of a man coughing and sputtering outside her chamber window. She got up and looked out the window to find him relieving himself on the ground with no interest in trying to find a modest location. Marion grinned to herself. What would her mother think if she knew her daughter was in such a situation? The woman would wail and make such a spectacle, demanding the man be chastised and Marion avert her gaze. Which she did, of course. There was nothing of interest to her in that man, though she did find humor in the situation and the fact that he did not know a lady had seen him.

The sun was just rising, and she hoped they would be on their way soon, so she got herself ready and repacked her chest then sat on it staring at the door, willing a knock to sound soon.

How long she sat there she did not know, but eventually a knock did sound, followed by Alexander's voice.

"My lady, are you ready?"

She opened the door and noticed how haggard his appearance was this morn. Dark circles encased his eyes, and his shirt, normally neat and perfectly in place, was wrinkled and had shifted slightly so the neckline was askew.

Serves him right for being such a boor.

She lifted her chin and said, "Aye, I am ready. My chest is there, and I am in want of sustenance."

"The carriage is ready and stocked with anything you might require, my lady. Neville shall retrieve your chest if you will follow me."

She followed him down the stairs and through the dining area of the inn which was vastly different than last eve. All the chairs were upside down and resting on the tables and a single servant girl quietly mopped the floors. She wondered briefly where that maid had been the night before. Alexander had spoken of the dangers to Marion, but did that extend to bar maids? Were they in danger too, or did the patrons usually not bother with them?

Alexander directed her to the carriage, and she was grateful when he closed the door and did not join her. He was true to his word. On the opposite seat was a basket filled with various pouches and a long stick of bread protruding over the side.

Once she settled herself, she reached into the basket and withdrew one pouch then thought again of the bar maid inside. Instead of opening the pouch, she reached into her pocket and withdrew some coin. She opened the carriage door and quickly stepped back inside the inn to find the maid.

"We have not met," she said upon locating her at the other end of the dining room. "But I imagine you work hard and so I would like to give this to you and let you know that I hope you are well and that you are noticed."

The young woman's eyes grew wide from Marion's first words and wider still when the coin was placed in her hands.

Marion folded the woman's fingers over the coin. "Keep this for yourself and do not let anyone know you have it. Do you promise?"

"Aye, my lady. I promise and thank ye."

"Very well, back to your business then."

Pleased with herself, she retreated to the carriage and closed the door before Alexander could say a word to her. For she was certain he would have some opinion on her actions—he usually did.

Back to the matter of the basket and its bounty and she was

far less guilty now for digging into it to see what treasures lay inside. Her stomach growled in appreciation as she opened a pouch to find a large piece of dark cake, the kind she loved with honey and loads of various fruits. She took a bite and loved the spicy flavors of cinnamon and cloves mixed with chewy cherries and apricots. There was comfort in those flavors which reminded her of the baking their cook did around Yuletide. Though it was late summer, she could picture strung garland and a deliciously roasting boar.

Marion sat back in her seat when she'd eaten her fill and sipped on the sweet mead that was fast becoming her favorite drink. She'd have to speak with her parents about it so that they could ask their brewer about it.

But it was the thought of returning so quickly to her parents that gave her pause. They'd been ecstatic at her prospects of traveling with the queen and spending more time with the earl. Her mother would no doubt be furious, but her father would come around, though be in no doubt disappointed.

They would both be surprised to see her. And with only a week or more to the summer season, they would return to Posso Tower within a fortnight.

And what then?

Would she ever see Alexander again? She was certain of her decision to remove herself from a situation that completely robbed herself of her agency. She wouldn't put up with that from anyone. But she couldn't imagine a way back from this and once she was home, why would their paths ever cross again?

That thought brought an ache into her heart. But he needed to understand that while some other suitors may have stayed and let him speak to them that way, she was not like them. Not one bit, and she had every intention of standing up to anyone who threatened her ability to feel safe.

Marion looked out through the carriage window as the sharp mountains turned to rolling hills as they journeyed east. A few times she dozed off only to jolt awake when the carriage dipped into a hole in the road. When she slept, she dreamed of a black rider and a masked dance partner. If only she could go back to those times and tell herself to be wary. She'd been so caught up in her attraction to him that she likely missed signs of the arrogance that was to come. And to think, she'd been warned off other men for the exact same attribute.

After a few hours riding, she found herself quite bored. Tired of mulling over the current predicament with Alexander, she realized she'd rather be arguing with him than sitting by herself stewing about it.

Without another thought, Marion reached up and knocked on the roof of the carriage. Moments later, it came to a stop. One of them hopped down from the driving seats and the door opened.

"Will you join me for the remainder of the journey?" she asked him.

His eyes narrowed for a moment before he nodded and entered, closing the door behind him. He moved the basket and then tapped the roof for the driver to continue. He positioned himself diagonal to her so that he could stretch out his long legs. Marion could only imagine how cramped it had been for him thus far and hoped he was a little more comfortable this way and here with her.

He stared at her without saying a word. Maybe that was best for the time being, for it appeared everything they'd said to one another in the past two days ended in a quarrel. She sat back with her hands folded in her lap and turned her attention to the passing scenery again. They didn't have to say anything just yet, and she was perfectly fine with the comfortable silence exchanged between them.

THE WOMAN WAS impossible to figure out. Why in Christ's name did she invite him to join her, and why was she now not saying anything? Did she think he was a mind reader? She was a confounding woman, and he was more and more confused as each moment passed.

When she'd tapped on the roof, he assumed she needed to relieve herself, but when she invited him to join her, he was certain she'd come to some grand decision.

Nay.

This was wholly unexpected, and he had to admit he didn't quite know what to make of it. But by God he would not open his mouth to speak first, and aye, he realized now that made him the stubborn one, but he would not contribute to whatever game this was that she played. He would just as soon now drop her off to her parents and be done with her.

Except that was contrary to how he felt about her. He still wanted to court and marry her and everything that went along with it. The previous day's events were unfortunate, and they just needed to get past it.

This new silence of hers was mind boggling to say the least.

Alexander followed her lead and turned to watch the countryside slip by. He'd much prefer to ride his horse than drive the carriage or ride inside. Thick woods eventually gave way to fields where crops flourished, or sheep grazed. There was a vast difference in the west highlands versus the east in terms of the landscape. Both were equally appealing to him, but nothing could stir his heart like the sharp peaks surrounding Glenshiel or the sight of the ancient Pictish brochs near Glenelg.

Or even his home. He loved every square inch of Inverary Castle, and its grounds and he couldn't imagine living anywhere else. And he had thought she would have been happy there. How wrong he'd been. In so many ways.

The truth was he had no idea how to fix it. Though he still wanted to, he was at a loss.

"You must be working your way through a very difficult puzzle, my lord," she said after what seemed like hours, but likely was only a few minutes.

"So, you do intend to speak to me," he said and instantly regretted it.

"I do not have to if you do not wish me to," she said and turned her head toward the window again.

Alexander shook his head and couldn't help but chuckle at the absurdity of their situation.

"Was the food to your satisfaction?"

She turned her head to look at the basket. A little redness appeared on her cheeks. Truly, it looked like a wild animal had rummaged through it.

"I did enjoy it," she said. "There is no shame in that," she said as she made to tidy it up.

"I did not mean anything by that or any other statement, Marion," he said.

"I never know what you mean, my lord. You say much and I am certain mean other things."

"That does not even make sense."

"I asked you to join me here so that we may both pass the time in a more pleasant manner," she said. "Not to quarrel with you."

"And I thank you for that kindness."

"Now, if you mentioned the basket because you are hungry and would like something, despite its appearance, there remains an abundance of selection. You are welcome to help yourself."

He'd only been looking for something to distract himself with, anything besides the thought of "a more pleasant manner" since those words had turned his thoughts to a very different path than what he was sure she had intended.

But now, he would take advantage of the opportunity to share in the small feast the cook had provided. There remained plenty of bread, sliced meat, cheese, and fresh apples. He'd filled his own wineskin with ale and so withdrew it from beneath his tunic and drank deeply.

"How much farther do you think before we reach Linlithgow?" she asked after he'd finished eating.

"A few hours yet, I suspect. 'Twill be nightfall likely before we arrive."

"And where are you to stay?"

He paused for a few moments. He'd not really thought of that, but was certain he would not be turned away at the palace even if the king and queen were not in residence. Other than that, he had some friends close by who he could call upon for their hospitality.

"I am sure we will have little trouble finding lodgings for the night."

"I will ask my father to put you up. We have plenty of room."

Well, that was unexpected. He wasn't sure how to respond considering the reason they were currently traveling was because she was so desperate to get away from him.

"That is very kind of you, but you need not go to any trouble. I know you are anxious to return to your family because of me."

Be damned if she didn't like him being direct. He'd been a boor yesterday, but he'd apologized and tried to make amends.

"It is no trouble, and I believe my parents would insist upon it considering the lengths you have taken to return me to my home when I needed to."

"And was it not my fault you *needed to* in the first place? Let us speak plainly, Lady Marion."

"That is my wish as well," she said.

"I was upset yesterday morn at the discovery of my sister and my steward. My reason was because of the deceit I perceived in their relationship. The one or the other should have come to me immediately as soon as it became apparent something was developing between them. But they chose to sneak around and keep it from me. Anyone at all could have discovered them and then we would have had to deal with the scandal of it."

"Do you so thoroughly oppose the match?"

"Nay, I do not. But the point is they are not yet married, and their discovery could have been ruinous for her."

"And does not the same sentiment apply to you and me?"

Why was he not surprised she would bring that up? "If you recall, Lady Marion, I had vowed not to let anything happen between us while courting."

She gasped. "Are you saying 'tis my own doing that we have shared intimacy?"

Christ, why did she always twist his words? "I am not saying that. I am answering your question in that the same sentiment should apply to you and me as well, but I cannot seem to keep my hands to myself or to stop imagining what it feels like to kiss you like I do right now."

He couldn't take it when her gaze dropped to his mouth. She had him in knots and if he didn't finish his train of thought, there would be no need to return her to her parents; he'd need to find a priest instead.

Alexander cleared his throat. "I was very upset when you came downstairs and discovered us and when I realized you would be able to figure out what was going on."

"Aye, plus Jean told me what was happening. Do you know she spoke of love?"

He sat back. He'd been so vexed with them both that he had not thought to ask either if intentions had been discussed.

"Considering how upset Jean was, I believe that to be the case and will need to return to Inverary to address them."

And that was it. He would need to leave her with her parents with no knowledge of when he would see her again.

"That does not explain why you took all your frustrations out on me and spoke to me like I would take that information and use it against you. That is much more difficult to forgive."

"Aye, you are correct. You have given me no reason to mistrust you, and again I am sorry for my reaction. It was not my intention to hurt you. I am unaccustomed to neither consulting nor commiserating with anyone when it comes to such matters. I do now know I could rely on you."

He purposely left the last part open-ended since he did not

want to drop her on her father's doorstep and never see her again. It took every ounce of strength for him to refrain from reaching across the carriage and pulling her to him.

"Then I accept your reasoning and your apology. Perhaps we should start over, my lord," she said.

It was an interesting suggestion. At least that way they would not need to be estranged to one another and there would be no formal good-bye.

"And the courtship? What is your opinion in that regard?"

"I believe you must do what should have been done in the first place."

"And what is that?"

"You should have spoken to my father and asked his permission."

He nodded and smiled. He would do just that.

CHAPTER SIXTEEN

THE CARRIAGE CAME to a halt, and she was relieved to be home at last. They had ridden in silence after their somewhat truce which left her a little bewildered and maybe hopeful. Her emotions had come full circle where he was concerned in the last two days, from excitement to indignance and back to admitting she had feelings for him.

At the front door, she reached up to unlatch, but her sister Alice was there before she could complete the task and swinging the door wide.

"What are you doing here? I thought you were with the king and the queen to see the earl?"

"Be easy, Alice. I am home, and the earl is with me."

She realized how that sounded immediately and, considering the lateness of the day, regretted Alice's obvious misinterpretation and excitement which bubbled out of her.

"Alice, who's there?" Her mother's voice preceded her from around the corner. "Marion! Why have you returned so quickly? Is aught amiss? Where is the queen? Where is the earl?"

Well, this wasn't starting out as she had hoped. "Mother, Alice, the earl is here." As she said this, she stepped to the side to reveal him.

"I needed to return home. Do not make assumptions, please, and the earl was gracious enough to see I was escorted properly."

Her mother's demeanor changed almost instantly upon seeing Alexander. "My dear earl, do come in and seat yourself at our table, for we are just about to seat for our evening meal."

"I do not wish to intrude upon your family," he said.

He, of course, would know how her mother would react to that and right on cue, she said, "Oh no, my dear, do come in and let us show you how grateful we are you kept our dear lass safe." She ignored Marion and took the earl's arm, practically dragging him to their small dining hall. "Do you know I have heard of these bands of highwaymen who would steal the eyes right out of your head. But they would not trouble one such as you…"

Her mother prattled on as Alice embraced her. "Whatever the reason, I am glad you have returned. Mother and Father have been relentless about my coming out next season and I fear they will be worse on me than they were on you."

She was not in the least surprised. Alice had been far too vocal about what she would and would not do and with whom she would converse. She'd set her sights high, and her parents would quite likely have to take her down a notch or two.

"Alice, please have Jonathan see to the earl's driver and ensure he is set up with a warm meal and a comfortable bed for the night."

"I shall, and then I want to hear every detail about your time away. Your lips are too tight for my liking," she said as she skipped away.

Marion drew a deep breath and joined her family and Alexander in the dining hall.

"…and I said to her that she should never have gotten mixed up in that family."

"Ahh, there's my wee lass," her father said and stood to embrace her. "Sit down by me and tell me of your travels. I had not expected to see you for more days than I was willing to count."

"Aye nor I, but a situation arose, and I felt it best if I returned to my family."

As she said this, she pointedly looked at Alexander whose

brow was knit again as he nodded at all the town's gossip her mother threw his way.

"A situation, you say?"

"Aye, and I believe the earl would like to have a conversation with you alone after dinner."

His brow shot up. "That sounds serious. Will I need my sword?"

Her father always had a way to break the tension with humor, but Marion was not entirely convinced this time that he was in jest.

"Nay, Father. He has a question to pose to you, and you should know already that my answer is aye. It is important to me that you be properly addressed in this matter."

"Then I shall bring my pocketbook."

"No need for that, either. You shall see for yourself when you have your discussion."

Marion settled into her meal then and worked hard to not devour the fish their cook had prepared exactly how Marion loved it. So tender and juicy. Though she would have loved to have two more pieces, she maintained her politeness and settled on the one with only an extra potato and bread.

She was as nervous as she'd ever been when it came to him. Starting over meant a full-on courtship that could go on for weeks or months and then a betrothal followed by another long wait before they married. She'd have to keep him at arm's length because even now, while he listened to her rambling mother, she wanted to sit on his lap and kiss him senseless.

Eventually the meal ended, and her father stood. "My lord Argyll, would you care to join me in my study?"

"Aye, my lord, I would like that very much."

The two men left the dining hall and after a short time, Marion could hear the door close. In her mind, she paced in front of it.

"Now, my dear, you have had a long journey as the earl has told me and so off to your chamber with you. I've asked a bath to be drawn, and you will be seen to and then into bed with you.

We will discuss your trip on the morrow when you're rested."

Two things drew questions in Marion's mind. The first was her surprise at the thought of the earl having gotten in any words at all. The second was that her mother had been polite in front of the earl, but a chastising was for certain on the way for cutting her trip short.

Uninterested in hearing anything of that nature this eve, Marion retreated to her chamber to where two servants she did not know poured steaming water into the wooden tub they used in their chambers when necessary. She dismissed the maids when the tub was full and removed her gown and shift and stepped into the glorious water. Leaning back, she let the full effect of the hot water sooth her aching bones.

What she would say to her mother on the morrow, she did not know, but for tonight she would try to rest her weary head. She felt like she'd been hit by a plank from the emotional turmoil. Had she done the right thing? She hoped so despite the racket she'd have with her mother. She did regret not speaking directly with the queen, but there was no way around that, and she sincerely hoped she would see the woman again and that she would forgive her.

Marion sat upright after a time. She'd just recalled something Jean had said just before their parting. Marion had been so upset she'd not let herself dwell on it until now.

Jean had said her brother loved Marion, but how could she know that? Aye, he'd been a brute, but he'd done everything since to try to make it up to her, and had he not dropped everything including a family crisis to see her to safety?

She mulled it over in her mind. For sanity's sake, he'd even left the king. Marion sank low into the water as if it could make her invisible. Did he love her? Did she love him? She couldn't imagine him kissing anyone else, that was for sure and certain. Further to that, she couldn't imagine anyone else kissing her.

What an outcome!

She loved him. She really did. She loved Alexander Campbell, and, on the morrow, she would tell him, for he would have to know before he returned to Inverary. She simply must.

There was no way she would sleep this night. She stepped out of the tub and donned her shift then sat near the fire to brush her hair. The nights were getting cooler now that the height of the summer had passed.

For what seemed like an age she stared into the fire until she heard a noise from outside below her window which faced the street.

Moving to peer outside, she saw Alexander step into the carriage and Neville turn it around to tear off up the street. He left! But what about his conversation with her father? Would he not have spoken to her to at least tell her it was all in place? Her heart sank in her chest as she sat on the side of the bed and let her tears flow. This was all her fault. Had she not been so impatient, she might still be at Inverary with him.

She'd lost him.

THE CONVERSATION WITH Marion's father had gone much better than he had hoped. The man was understanding that they had begun their courtship and appeared pleased that he had sought the approval of the king at least. He'd been forthcoming as to the reason Marion had wished to return and to their desire to begin a formal courtship anew.

But that was not what he wanted.

And her father was far more intuitive than he'd given the man credit. So, they'd agreed on bypassing the courtship and betrothal and that Alexander could begin planning the wedding which was his wish.

He'd left her father with the task of informing no one, not even his wife—especially not his wife—and that Alexander would return the following day with the particulars and to formally propose to Marion.

Her father did not hesitate and appeared pleased that he knew something his wife did not. Well, he'd leave them to that bit, but for now he would make his way to the palace and hopefully secure the king's blessing for them to marry at Linlithgow Abbey. He did not want to wait one more day to make her his. The more he thought of it, the more he was convinced they were perfect for each other even in the way they quarreled.

Alexander pulled up to the palace. The hour was late, but he was immediately admitted entry and was informed the king and queen were expected in the morning, having cut the tour short, but that he would be welcome to one of the guest bed chambers in their apartments. He agreed and didn't even mind the lengths to which the king's servants went to ensure his comfort.

Now sitting in a steaming tub of lavender and rose scented water, he thought of the details that would need to be secured in order for them to marry. His family would not be in attendance, but they would rectify that as soon as they returned to Inverary. He would need to see a tailor in the morning to see to some new clothes which he hoped they could expedite. Considering the end of the summer, he supposed the local tailors would be happy for the business.

Aye, hopefully the father could keep it from the mother as he did not want her to spoil it for Marion, and he wanted his future bride to find out from him and no one else. He leaned back in the tub and smiled at the thought of asking her to marry him now in but a few days' time.

Each time a sparkle of doubt entered his mind, he swiftly pushed it away. This was right; he knew it in every fiber of his being. She was his, and she would soon be his countess. The title would fit her. His family would fit her.

The hours would not pass fast enough until he was with her again and she was agreeing to be his bride.

Alexander exited the tub and brushed the water from his body before crawling into bed to find some slumber, but his thoughts were on nothing but her and she would not let him rest. Visions of her beautiful face danced across his mind, leaving his heart racing and his body tight with need.

The next morning, he dressed early and stopped by the tailor to deal with that business while he waited for the king's arrival. The tailor promised his final garments the day after tomorrow, so that would be the date he would want the wedding. He could barely contain himself as he returned to the palace and was grinning ear to ear when the king rode into the courtyard on his horse.

"You are much more chipper than the last time I saw you, Argyll," he said as he dismounted and stepped over to greet him.

"Aye, Your Majesty, and once again I am grateful for your understanding and support."

"I do support you, Argyll. You have become a friend to me as Lady Marion has become a friend to my wife. She treasures her above all others, and I want only what is best for you both."

"And you harbor no ill will at the manner in which I left? I have lamented on it."

"I do not. As much as I enjoyed our short time at Inverary, I am much more suited to the entertainment in my own court."

Alexander wondered as much and was grateful for the king's candor.

"Now that is sorted, I have a favor to ask," Alexander said.

The king shook his head. "You do not need favors from me. Whatever it is you want, you shall have."

"I wish to marry Lady Marion the day after tomorrow in the abbey."

The king grinned. "Two days, hey. Someone is anxious."

"Aye, that I am. There is no need to wait any longer. I am certain of my feelings for her."

"And are you certain of her feelings for you? I do not wish to cast doubt, but the last I heard, she wanted to be as far away from you as possible."

He was not certain, but he would be. And he trusted his heart which told him she would agree, and if she did not yet love him, she would in time. Of that he was certain.

"Aye, I am certain."

The king peered up at the palace and then around the space in the courtyard. "Two days, you say," he said and looked back to Alexander. "I can work with that."

At that moment, the queen's carriage arrived and the king moved to open her door. When she emerged and spied Alexander, she smiled genuinely.

"It is very good to see you, my lord. I trust my friend is well?"

"Aye, Your Majesty. She is well."

"And she is about to become much better when our man here asks for her hand in marriage. Dear wife, it appears we have two days to plan a wedding. Are you up for the task?"

The queen clasped her hands together and laughed. "I am indeed, as this is the most glorious news I could have heard upon our return. You must tell me everything. How will you propose? What are her favorite flowers? Does she prefer fish or meat? You must bring her to my apartment this afternoon so we may fit her for a gown."

"Now, now, wife. We shall ensure we have plenty of everything Lady Marion enjoys. We must release our friend so that he may go and ask the lady first."

"Oh," she said. "Right you are. We will need to check our mead stores, and I will have a peacock styled cake for her; she loves the white one..."

The queen moved away from them as she spoke to no one in particular but walked in the direction of the hall. Once the servants saw her, they rushed to her, and she sent them off to find various things.

"She will enjoy this task," the king said. "Thank you for including us."

"Your Majesty does not need to thank me. We are blessed to have your patronage."

"And that you have. Now off you go to your bride. Godspeed."

Alexander was as nervous as a schoolboy upon arrival at their manor house. He dismounted and tossed the reins to their servant and straightened his attire before knocking on the door.

A young maid opened the door and waited for him to announce himself.

"Please tell the lord of the house Alexander Campbell is here to see him."

She nodded and permitted him entry. "Wait here, m'lord," she said in a quiet, youthful voice that almost sounded like she was singing.

Marion's father exited his study, and as soon as he saw Alexander, ushered him inside, all the while looking about. He was giggling like wee Archie when he closed the door.

"They don't know," he said and clapped his hands.

Alexander was moved by the man's enthusiasm. He was clearly pleased with himself at having kept the secret.

"The ladies have all gone to the morning market, but are due back at any moment. I have been worried you would have encountered them."

"Nay, I have been to the tailor and to the king. He has agreed for the marriage to take place at the abbey, and I cannot comment on the preparations for a feast since they both jumped to that conclusion quickly and appeared to be excited at the prospect of throwing a wedding feast."

The king in particular was more enthusiastic than Alexander had presumed. "That is very generous of their majesties. Now we only have one piece of business to discuss, my lord, and that is of Marion's dowry."

Alexander had forgotten all about it and in truth would take her for no dowry, but that would be insulting to the family.

"I have ten thousand marks set aside for Marion. I do hope that number is suitable to you."

"Aye, my lord, that is more than agreeable to me."

Alexander did not want to belabor the point as it made him a little uneasy taking money to marry a woman he loved.

"Very well then, it is settled."

They shook hands just as the front door opened and closed, and Alexander could hear a young woman and Marion's mother arguing over some sort of hat. A soft knock sounded at the door and a moment later, Marion entered but then stopped with her jaw slack when she locked gazes with him.

CHAPTER SEVENTEEN

ARION'S BREATH CAUGHT in her throat. What was *he* doing here? She'd practically given up on ever seeing him again. She shifted her gaze from Alexander to her father and back again. Both men wore an odd smile that she could not decipher.

"Do come in and close the door, daughter."

She did as he asked and moved to sit in a chair across from them both. She tried to steady her breath as much as she could, but her insides jittered around like a box of butterflies had just been unleashed.

"I imagine you are curious as to why I have come this morning?"

"Aye, my lord, as I witnessed you leaving last eve. I did not think you would return." As she said this, a lump formed in her throat. She was of the opinion she'd cried all her tears the night before, and in fact had cried herself to sleep. She'd been grateful for the distraction of the morning market, but now he was before her, all those emotions came flooding back and tears welled in her eyes. She blinked them away and cast her eyes downward, not wanting him to see.

Large warm hands reached for hers as he knelt before her. He squeezed them and said, "Marion, I am not going anywhere." His voice was but a whisper.

She looked up to meet his gaze and saw tears in his as well. "I love you, Marion. I believe now I always have, and I want to marry you. I left last eve after I acquired your father's permission to seek the king's permission for us to marry at the abbey."

"The abbey, as in Linlithgow Abbey?"

He nodded. "The very one. As you can imagine, the queen and king are now planning a wedding feast the likes this region has rarely seen."

"So, what you are telling me is that I cannot refuse," she said, trying an attempt at a jest. It was all so overwhelmingly what she wanted, she could hardly trust it.

He sat back and released her hands. "Do you want to refuse me?" he asked in a quiet voice.

She shook her head and reached for his hands. "I do not want to refuse you, my lord. I do want to marry you. I do."

He was on his feet in an instant and pulled her up with him. He picked her up and twirled her around then planted her firmly on her feet.

"Then it is set. We will marry the day after tomorrow and I have much to see to before then." Turning to her father, he said, "I trust you will arrange for her to arrive at the queen's apartments this afternoon for her fitting?"

"My fitting?"

"Aye, the queen has insisted upon it."

Marion was not sure how she felt about the idea of an elaborate gown, but she would be pleased to see her friend again and appreciated her generosity. Now she could apologize to her in person for her abrupt departure from Inverary.

Alexander cupped her face with his hands and brushed his lips across hers. Out of the corner of her eye, she noticed that her father had turned away to inspect the curtains.

Focusing her attention back to him, she returned the kiss, soft and sweet. "Is this real?" she asked.

"Aye, love. 'Tis real."

"But your family are not here."

"Not to worry about my family. We will celebrate with them

upon our return to Inverary."

She hadn't thought about that. She'd have to say goodbye to her family for good. Not that she would change her mind, but she had simply not considered where they would live.

"Is that acceptable to you, Marion? Will you be my countess and live with me at Inverary Castle?"

Imagining living there with him was easy. But it was all happening so fast her heart was moving along faster than her mind. In this matter, her heart would guide her, and her mind would have to catch up in time.

"Aye, Alexander. I will be your countess and live with you at your beautiful home."

He embraced her again and then kissed her on the forehead. "I will see ye in two days at the abbey. Enjoy being pampered by the queen as it is clear this wedding has brought her much joy."

Marion laughed. "Aye, I imagine planning an elaborate event upon short notice is something both she and the king enjoy."

Alexander released her then shook her father's hand and left.

When the door closed, she plopped down on the chair and drew a deep breath then let it whoosh from her lips.

"Are ye certain of this, lass?" her father asked as he sat near her.

"Aye, father. 'Tis a wee bit sudden, but he is a good man."

"And do ye love him?"

That her father would ask her that when her mother wouldn't was the distinct difference between them. She was sure her mother cared for her wellbeing, but she was less concerned with feelings and more with duty—unlike her father.

"Aye, I love him."

"Then let us tell your mother and get ye ready to be doted on by a queen no less. My daughter, a favorite of the queen," he said and shook his head. "For all your balking over the years about marriage, I never imagined such a wonderful outcome. I have spoken at length with the man and have formed a high opinion of him."

"I have as well," she said, not daring to share just how familiar she was with the earl.

"Very well, go and call in your mother."

Marion found her mother in the front room that had the best light for her needlepoint. She did not look up when Marion entered, but Alice, ever the astute one, narrowed her eyes toward Marion.

"Something has happened," she said. "Mother, look at Marion. Something has happened."

Her mother looked up and squinted at Alice then Marion. "Don't be foolish, Alice. The earl has gone away. What could have possibly happened?"

"Mother, Father would like to see you in his study. It is a matter of some import."

Her mother placed her needlepoint in her lap and regarded Marion more decidedly, her brows drawn together in perpetual dissatisfaction with any goings on that did not include needlepoint or betrothals for her daughters.

"Very well, I will go see him, but it had better be important."

Marion led her mother to the study and opened the door to let her pass through. She was not sure if her constitution could handle her mother's reaction, but at the same time it would not be fair for her to leave her father to deal with her alone.

After closing the door, Marion moved to stand by her father and clasped his hand while her mother took a seat in front of them.

"Well, out with it. I have my stitching to finish."

Her father flicked his hand toward her mother as if to dismiss what she said. "Never mind your stitching, woman. As we speak, a wedding is being planned for our daughter at the abbey with a feast to follow at the palace."

For the first time in Marion's seventeen years, she was surprised her mother had no words. The sight of her wide-eyed expression and slack jaw was almost humorous. Marion had to work to not burst into laughter.

"Did you hear me, wife? Our daughter is to be married in two days. I thought you would be joyous over this news."

Her mother blinked a couple of times and mouthed, "who?"

"I am to marry the Earl of Argyll," she said and watched as her mother slowly shifted her attention from her husband to her daughter.

She drew in a deep breath and in the next instant a sound emanated from her that surely only dogs could hear. The sound was so high pitched that Alice came barreling through the door wearing a look of pure fright.

"What is amiss?"

"Nothing, sister. I am getting married is all and our mother is processing the information." Marion moved to her mother and took her hands then shook them a little to bring her back to the moment.

"You are marrying the earl?"

"Aye, Mother, I am."

"The nice earl who we thought was lost to you?"

"The very one."

"And you will need a dress, and other clothes," she said as a little pink rose in her cheeks when she flicked her gaze to her husband. "And we will need to have a talk."

"All is in hand, mother. The queen has arranged for her seamstresses to create a gown for me. We must make haste with our midday meal as the queen is expecting us this afternoon for my fitting."

With that, her mother scurried around the house looking for bits and bobs of things Marion did not comprehend as she had an entire conversation with herself about whatever she gathered. Something about a grandmother's pin and something else about a bonnet.

Within the hour, they were fed and dressed in their best gowns and in the carriage heading toward the palace. Alice was permitted to go because there would only be women in attendance, and it was clear her mother was not up for the battle that would ensue if she were to remain at the manor house.

Marion drew in a deep breath as they approached the palace. The last time she was here, she had no idea she would return under these circumstances.

THE TAILOR WAS more than adept at his craft. Alexander was amazed how quickly he had produced the outline of a thick velvet doublet and trews. He was not partial to hose and, as such, had his long boots polished to a shine. He spent the remainder of that day and the next traveling back and forth between the tailor for fittings and reining in the king for his elaborate plans. The man was determined to not be outdone and so had hired workmen to build wall-to-wall trellises that would be filled with as many flowers from their gardens as they could spare. He further had secured one of the gardeners who had an interest to capture and safely secure as many butterflies as they could find, even if it meant traveling to gardens in the surrounding areas.

While he was appreciative of the effort, he tried to make the king see that he and his wife were not the kind of people who needed such a spectacle. The challenge was the delicate delivery of such a message.

In the end, he did not question the king any further, rather enjoyed the man's enthusiasm for decorative detail. Everywhere he looked in the great hall he could see the vision coming together. Between florists and workmen, there were the lutenists who were deciding where they should be situated, which sometimes conflicted with the wishes of the makars. All he could do was stand aside and watch it come together.

No detail was too small for the king's attention, and Alexander found himself most of the time with nothing more to do than step out of someone's way.

"Argyll! What do you think?" the king said from beside him as he clapped his hands together.

"You have truly outdone yourself, Your Majesty. I could not imagine how quickly 'tis all coming together."

"It is not my first event, my friend," he said with a wink then strode off to direct the workmen and florists. He was not their king in that moment, expecting heads to bow and knees to bend in curtsy; rather he was a director pulling everyone together for the show. And what a show it would be.

As Alexander made to return to the tailor for another fitting, he spied a carriage pulling up in the outer courtyard. Curious, he waited to see who would emerge. He smiled when the wind pulled her red tresses out before she could step out. Alexander waited until she noticed him before he raised his hand to her in greeting.

She walked toward him wearing a shy grin and looking down as much as she met his gaze.

"Is aught well?" he asked.

"Aye, my lord, and you?"

"Aye, all is well with me, although," he said and turned to look at the entrance to the great hall and then back to her, "I believe the king is having far too much enjoyment planning this feast."

"I can say much the same about the queen. Her vision for my gown is such that I do not believe you would find me within the layers of fabric without a map."

"That sounds to me like an enjoyable challenge," he said, leaning close to her.

Her cheeks grew red as she smiled and looked down.

"I do hope you have been able to assert your wishes to her in a delicate manner," he said.

"I have and I believe we have come to a perfect marriage of our styles."

"I am glad to hear it and am off for my final fitting with the tailor," he said and then reached for her hand. He kissed it and said, "Tomorrow you and I will be wed, and we shall be the focus of much attention. But once that has passed, our life will be much like we experienced in my home. I do believe that is agreeable to you."

"It is very agreeable to me, my lord. I enjoyed your home far more than this lavishness. But I do not wish to offend my friend."

"I agree. Now to one other matter," he said and leaned in close to her ear. His hot breath sent a decadent shiver down her body.

"And what is that?" she asked a little breathless at his nearness.

"I cannot wait to hear you call my name when I bring you pleasure."

With that and leaving her a little unsteady on her feet, he grinned as he walked back to his horse and mounted. He took his time riding to the tailor's to enjoy the moment and not let the whole urgency of planning and making the wedding occur so quickly offset the gravity of what he was about to do.

All doubt had now passed out of him. He was more certain of this decision than any other in his life, right to the very fiber of his being.

His only regret was that his family would not bear witness, and he had no idea if Alain had decided to await his return or leave entirely. He prayed it was not the latter for he wanted to sit with him and Jean and work out their intentions and see how he could support them.

But if Alain had left, he would not blame him, and he would accept any decision Jean made for her own future. In the spirit of his own happiness with his situation, he found himself wanting the same perfect match for those he cared about as well.

And Marion was his perfect match. In every way. He shifted on his horse at the thought of her writhing beneath him as he would pleasure her. He had to push those thoughts away if he was to get through the remainder of this day and evening.

As he arrived at the tailor's, he secured his horse and noticed a few more people about than he expected. When he entered, he could see that the place was quite busy with the workers buzzing about like bees in springtime.

To his tailor, John, he asked, "What is happening?"

John looked exhausted, but wore a gentle smile all the same. "Word has gotten out about your nuptials, and every man in town wants to see the deed done even if they are not invited to the feast. Truly, we are now out of everything we had pre-made that could be adjusted for the average build as well as our demonstration pieces. And they keep coming," he said with a shaky laugh. "My wee shop has never seen so many people in it at the one time and I can only hope the floorboards can withstand the abuse."

Alexander appreciated the quiet man's bewilderment and dry sense of humor, and felt a little responsible for springing this on him with such short notice.

"Is there aught I may do to assist?"

"Nay, m'lord. I will bring you back now for your final fitting and leave this gaggle to my staff."

Alexander looked over his shoulder one last time at the fine gentlemen lifting scarves and calling out numbers as though they were haggling over a lower price, but rather they were seeking to outbid one another for the final pieces of fabric in the shop. When all was said and done, John would be able to boast a fair haul of coin for his troubles. That understanding gave Alexander comfort and eased his guilt enough so that he could settle into the next couple of hours while John finished his outfit. Normally, the work would be done in various stages, but the agreement included final measurements and sewing at the same time, so Alexander would leave the shop with his final product in tow. He was pleased with John's workmanship and would ensure he was appropriately compensated.

He hoped Marion was enjoying her process, but mostly he thought about how enjoyable it would be to remove the clothing that was currently being tucked and snipped to perfectly fit and accentuate her bountiful curves. And he couldn't wait to explore each and every one.

CHAPTER EIGHTEEN

MARION BLINKED HER eyes a couple of times and looked around to find her bearings. She sat upright in her bed and rubbed her eyes as she tried to figure out where she was. After a few moments, she awoke enough to recall she'd been offered a chamber in the queen's apartment after a long day and evening of fittings.

She could scarcely believe she would be marrying Alexander that day. Yet here she was, having spent a day and a half being fawned over by the queen and her seamstresses who were surely bewitched by magical powers considering how quickly they brought her gown together. She would quite literally be sewn into it this morning with clear instructions as to how the maids were to get her out of it later. The queen had also insisted on several options for her wedding night, each making the heat rise even more to her cheeks. She finally settled on a couple that balanced the naughtiness envisioned each time he was near with a respectable amount of modesty.

Moments later, a knock sounded at the door followed by a slew of servants carrying a copper tub with buckets of steaming water. She was to be scrubbed from head to toe and her hair set in cloth strips to dry so as to encourage long loose curls. The queen had suggested she wear a more modern hood, but Marion was firm she would wear her hair down and uncovered until she absolutely had to cover it.

Laying back in the steaming water, she thought about her mother and the item she had given together with its significance. The pin she'd brought was made of silver in the shape of a gryphon head and for its eye a red ruby. She had shown it to the queen who knew just how to incorporate it onto the neckline of Marion's gown, which was a light-green soft velvet on which the brooch would surely stand out.

Marion let the maids lift her arms to wash then pour more water over her. She sat up as her hair was washed and rinsed. The whole experience was so soothing she wondered why she didn't partake more often. Though she supposed she didn't normally self-indulge as a rule.

Before long, she was out of the tub, dried off, and sat by the fire wearing a thick velvet robe while the maids took the time to roll her hair around each piece of fabric then tie it atop her head. By the time they were done, her neck hurt from trying to keep her head straight.

While she waited, she was brought a platter with a light meal and a tankard of her favorite mead to sustain her until the evening feast which she was told would be far more elaborate than that for the tournament the king had recently held. She recalled her first impression of the courtyard and the mounds of pastries. How they could possibly outshine that on such short notice, she had no idea, but she was excited to find out.

The door opened and in bounded her sister in a lovely blue velvet gown with her hair twisted into ringlets and a gold wreath with little white pearls on her head. She twirled in a circle and then stopped.

"Well?"

"You look a vision, sister," Marion said. She would no doubt catch the attention of those gathered between her pretty blonde hair and outgoing personality.

"I do look a vision, don't I?" she said as she twirled again.

"Where is Mother?"

"She is fussing over the boys and sent me here to help you get ready. Though I think she did not want me underfoot."

Marion could believe it. The two younger boys were a menace when they did not want to get ready for church. She could only imagine the havoc they would wreak when having to dress in even more formal clothes. She nearly giggled at the thought of them wearing hose. Her brother's leg had healed enough so he could walk now with a crutch, and he was not happy about having to be careful.

"You look beautiful, Marion," Alice said in an uncharacteristic somber tone. "I will miss you when you leave us."

Marion turned to her and reached for her hands. "Here," she said as she pulled up a chair and drew Alice toward it. "You may come and visit me whenever you like, though I think you will not miss me so much as you will be planning your own coming out next year. I heard Mother and Father agree they would not make you wait."

"Aye," she said with a mischievous grin. "I kept on them until I wore them down. I used all their arguments for you against them and they vowed to never speak about such matters with more than one of their children present at any given time."

"You are too clever for your own good, sister. Someday someone will use that against you and then you will learn your own lessons the hard way."

"But the difference between you and me, my lady soon to be countess, is that I know I am cleverer than most men. And that is how I know I will not end up with the wrong one."

"Well, I sincerely hope you keep your wits about you. I have met some very unworthy people in this sphere who sidle up to you as a friend, only to toss you aside for their own benefit."

"Excellent. Maybe I will find some who are worthy of the battle."

"The battle?"

"Aye, sister. You do not get it at all, do you?"

"I admit, I do not know what you mean at all."

Alice drew a deep breath. "I envision the king's court like a battlefield. There are those who are pawns who are sent in first to get things started, and then there are those who will be most affected by how the battle plays. And then there are those who orchestrate the final outcome. And I, for one, cannot wait to partake."

"Exactly how is it you know so much about the king's court that you have devised this elaborate analogy?"

Alice was clever, but this was even far beyond her imaginings.

"I have listened to our parents and particularly our mother plot her schemes in order to find suitable matches for us. But it wasn't until Father Connor spoke of good and evil in the form of a battle that I really pieced it all together. It is but a game, sister. You were fortunate enough to find a match with someone who, like you, despised that game."

Marion shook her head and laughed. "You are too wise for your own good, Alice."

"I know it," she said as she stood to go look out the window.

The lass didn't have a modest bone in her body and Marion was certain she would not only acquire the upper hand in her future relationships, but she felt almost sorry for those who would enter into her arena.

After a time, the maids returned and checked her hair which was not fully dry. They untied all the fabric which released each perfectly formed tress. They pulled and tugged at it until it hung in long curls flowing down her back. She was to wear a thin silver tiara offered to her by the queen which matched her brooch in style and shape.

The door opened again and in came the pieces of her dress. She disrobed and raised her arms for first her shift and then a thicker skirt that would be tied around her waist. They pulled her arms through the bodice and tied that tight at her back which resulted in her breasts rising and showing deep cleavage.

Next was the outer piece that would need to be laced into the inner garments. She was relieved that they had found a solution to sewing her into the garment, for she anticipated Alexander's impatience once they were to retire later that evening. She bit the inside of her cheek to not laugh at the vision of a frustrated and aroused Earl of Argyll. Never mind that she was certain she would be just as anxious.

Once the skirt was laced into her inner garments, they drew her arms into the top bodice which was then laced to the bottom and up the back with a flap to hide the connection. The sleeves were fitted down her arms to the elbow and then flowed to the floor. Her neckline was just above her inner bodice and left little to the imagination, so they tucked a sheer scarf into the front on one side, around her neck, and then into the other side on the front. This would help for modesty for anyone not standing beside her, but Alexander would have quite the view once they stood at the altar.

And there she stood, before the mirror with her slack-jawed sister standing beside her, wondering if she'd ever felt so pleased with her appearance.

The only thing left to do now was to marry an earl.

ALEXANDER ADJUSTED HIS fur-lined cape so that it covered most of his left shoulder, leaving the design of his dark-blue brocade doublet visible on his right. He fidgeted until he got it looking the way he wanted. His cape was longer than a typical mantle, but not as long as a full cape. The fine embroidery on his leine was visible from underneath his doublet, and as he spied himself in the mirror, he became satisfied finally with his appearance.

His hair was shorter than many men of the time who often wore it tied at their nape, but he found that uncomfortable and so he wore it slightly shorter than his shoulders. He'd trimmed his beard so the shape would be clean, but he could not bear to have his face fully shaved and so kept it light.

And now there was nothing left but to put her ring in his pocket and make his way to the abbey. The king's jeweler had several styles he could select from and in the end, he chose a band of intertwined white and yellow gold in the form of a Celtic knot. He would have something designed for her for later, but for today, he would honor her with this one.

Now standing near the Archbishop of St. Andrew's no less, Alexander stilled his nerves and waited as patiently as he could for the first sight of his bride.

The abbey was as full as he imagined it could ever be as, true to their word, people had come from all over to witness these nuptials.

The king's lutenists played their solemn hymns quietly until they were signaled to increase the volume and tempo.

And then he saw her. This vision in pale green with hair like flame and a tiara that sparkled as the sunlight hit it when she passed by the high arched windows of the abbey.

No one made a sound as she walked toward him with her father to her right and her holding a thick bouquet of hawthorne. This pleased him so, since she could have chosen the most exotic flower from the king's gardens, but instead she chose a flower native to Scotland and as hardy as her people.

He met her gaze as they neared. She was more beautiful than any woman he'd ever beheld and even more beautiful than even she was before this moment. His breath caught in his throat as her father placed her hand in his.

He mouthed "beautiful," which brought color to her cheeks and that shy smile he was coming to adore on her face.

The archbishop said some words and offered blessings, but Alexander could focus on none of it. All he could see was this glorious woman before him and envision the life they were about to embark on together. He could see them expanding the gardens at Inverary, their many children, and he could even see them growing old together. In a flash their entire lives played out behind his eyes, and his heart ached with love for her so much it hurt.

The archbishop instructed Alexander to place his ring on her finger then joined their hands together.

"Alexander, Earl of Argyll and Chieftain of Clan Campbell, will you take this woman to be your wife?"

"I will," he said.

"Marion, will you take this man to be your husband?"

"I will," she said.

"Now let us humbly invoke God's blessing upon this bride and groom, that in his kindness he may favor with his help those on whom he has bestowed the Sacrament of Matrimony. By the power vested in me by His Holiness the Pope of the Holy Catholic Church, I pronounce thee husband and wife."

Alexander didn't hear another word. He reached for Marion and cupped her face with his hands and brushed the softest kiss on her lips as prudence would dictate. He'd make up for that later. And he also recalled a conversation about her gown being sewn onto her. They would have to repair it on the morrow for he was not about to waste one second on her gown once they were alone later.

For the moment, he could not wait for her to see the great hall and how perfectly it had been transformed not into a garish affair with overly ornate decoration, but something elegant and soft, just like her.

"Fare thee well, Countess?"

She squeezed his arm where she held it as they walked down the aisle of the abbey and nodded at the various nobles and commonfolk who had come to bear witness.

"Aye, my lord. I am very well."

"I am pleased to hear it and am looking forward to your impression of the great hall. I believe you will find it much transformed from the last time you were here. And by the way, I am very pleased that your tastes won out regarding your gown and choice of decoration. I shall do my best not to cause it too much harm later."

Her fingers dug even harder into his arm.

"My lord, you need not worry about the gown. The seamstress devised a solution for ease of removal."

It was everything he could do not to stare at her as they continued on down the impossibly long aisle, nodding and smiling at attendees.

"I am not certain if I am relieved or disappointed."

"Are you saying you wanted to damage my garment?"

"I believe I was prepared for the challenge, aye. But truth be told, I am counting down the moments until I have you alone and we can explore one another for many—long—hours."

Her hand on his arm was like a death grip now and he was left in no doubt she was as affected by him. Their joining would be jointly enjoyed; he would ensure it.

"My lord, I believe you have stirred me to the point of distraction."

He sucked in his breath. He deserved that as his loins tightened at her admission. Aye, he would need to desist lest they both make a spectacle of themselves before all these witnesses. They were to witness the nuptials, not the consummation!

"My lady, I promise to behave myself until such time as we are alone, as long as you do not do that thing with your eyes watching my mouth. If you do, all bets are off, and I will fling you over my shoulder and carry you off to our chamber without a care who is offended."

He chuckled when she sucked in her breath. Oh, but it was growing painfully clear they had the capacity to drive one another to distraction, and upon her knowledge of lovemaking, he was not sure he would be able to remain in control of their passions. A part of him was wary of relinquishing control, but another very visceral part longed for it—for her to command him and be free with her needs.

Christ, would this aisle never end?

But eventually it did. He led her to the walkway to enter the courtyard and onward to the great hall. He wanted her to see it before anyone else arrived so had requested they all remain in the abbey for a few moments until he could let her take it all in.

They ascended the steps and turned the corner, and when they did, she gasped and placed her hand on her heart. She looked to him with tears welling in her eyes.

"Please tell me those are tears of joy and not abhorrence."

"How did you make this happen? What sort of magic could offer such a transformation?"

"It was all the king's doing. You have him to thank. I merely tried to illustrate the difference in our preferences."

He was pleased the king had clearly listened. The entire walls were covered in white and pale pink flowers of many variations, but the effect was as though the hall sat in the middle of a garden. Each table was adorned with bouquets of similar flowers of the same palette, but protruding from them were feathers shaped to resemble a white peacock. The head table was dressed in pine garlands decorated with roses, thistle, and a touch of the design in the hall. Butterflies flitted about the flowers, giving a faerie-like visage.

"Alexander, 'tis the most beautiful thing I have ever seen," she said and turned to him, a small tear rolling down one cheek.

He placed his hands on her shoulders and kissed her forehead, each cheek, and then her lips.

"You are more beautiful than anything here. Do you know you have made me the happiest man in all of Scotland—nay, the world this day? I love you, my sweet countess."

They stood there for a few moments longer in an embrace, looking at the sight before them, holding onto the moment before the crowd would descend and the celebrations commence.

CHAPTER NINETEEN

Between the music and the feast and the overall joviality, Marion had plenty to distract her from the man sitting beside her. Except that it didn't. She was keenly aware of every inch of him and each movement he made. He'd moved his foot so that it rested alongside hers, and he was now leaning on the arm of the chair so that his arm touched hers. Her skin tingled where they touched.

"Are you enjoying the feast?" he asked in a low deep voice that sent shivers through her.

A part of her wanted the evening to last forever, but a much more visceral part, that part of her as a woman who knew instinctively what she wanted from a man, wanted him to fling her over his shoulder and carry her off to their bed.

Their bed.

Marion turned to him and mustered up whatever courage she could find.

"I am, my lord. But I am hungry for something else."

She almost giggled as the words came out of her mouth at the sight of his eyes dropping to her lips and back to meet her gaze. He drew a shaky breath and leaned in close to her ear.

"Do you wish to leave the hall?"

His hot breath on her neck made her belly tighten and wetness pool between her legs. What did she want? She wanted to feel his skin on hers. She wanted him kissing her everywhere and most of all, she didn't want anyone to bear witness to the wantonness that conflicted her.

"Do you think our hosts will be offended if we leave the feast early?"

"I am certain they will understand."

Alexander turned to speak with the king and then back to her.

In a low voice, he said, "The king said he is surprised we are still here."

In the next moment, the king was on his feet and addressing those gathered.

"My lords and ladies, I urge you to raise your cups as we celebrate this joyous union of two loyal houses. To the earl and his new countess, slainte!"

A booming, "Slainte!" erupted from the crown as Alexander pushed back his chair and held out his hand for her.

Marion took his hand and together they left the hall to much applause echoing through the hall. They walked slowly through the courtyard and onward to their chamber, each step loosing more sensations within her body.

The only thing stabilizing her was his warm hand holding hers. She was grateful for the silence as they ascended the stairs, as she didn't trust her voice and she didn't want him to think the shaking that would surely be present in her voice was from hesitation.

Outside of their chamber door, he placed his hands on her shoulders and turned her toward him. For a few heartbeats, he merely gazed upon her without speaking, making the tension within her draw even tighter.

"Are you cold?" he asked.

"Nay, Alexander, I am not cold."

She was rather the exact opposite.

"I want to tell you something, but I do not really know how."

Icicles of dread crept into her heart.

"What is it?" she whispered.

He opened the door and waited until she was inside before closing it.

"My passion for you," he whispered, "is so strong, I fear—"

Alexander stepped back from her for a moment and raked his hands through his hair.

"What is it you fear?" she asked as she took a step toward him.

"I do not wish to hurt you, but it will be your first time, and it may be unavoidable."

Waves of relief washed through her. She feared he was about to tell her he did not really want her or some such madness her tortured mind had created in the moment. Marion drew in a deep breath. She did not want half of him, just the reserved bit. She wanted to experience his passion unleashed as she wished to do with hers.

So, she did the only thing she could think of. She turned around and asked, "Will you untie my bodice, my lord?"

She smiled as she heard him draw a deep breath and step to her. He pushed her hair over one shoulder and kissed her neck as he tugged at the strings beneath her bodice. She was pleased he didn't have to ask how or where the ties were located.

Marion imagined there were various kinds of torture one could endure while waiting for pleasure, but she had to admit to herself she had never known any such as this, as with each movement of Alexander undressing her, his lips found a new and more potent spot on her neck.

When her bodice and skirt were on the floor, he turned her around and reached for the fine ribbon that held her shift together above her breasts. He gazed deeply into her eyes as he pulled it, letting loose the knot and allowing him to slowly open it so that he could slide her shift down her shoulders. Her hard nipples were the only thing keeping the garment from falling to the floor. Alexander placed his thumbs on them and drew tantalizing circles, making her body pulse in ways she'd never known possible.

Her head fell backward as he squeezed one nipple and reached to the small of her back to press her hard against him. His hot mouth on her neck and hard body tight to hers was her undoing. Marion dove her fingers into his hair and drew his head upward to find his mouth. She kissed him with such abandon, seeking and finding his tongue for a dance like he'd done with her before.

In the next instant, he hoisted her so that her legs straddled him as he carried her to the bed. Laying atop her, he drew her shift to below her breasts and cupped one, squeezing hard. Marion's body bucked upward as jolts of pleasure washed through her body. Every movement he made brought her higher and higher on a plane she could not understand nor fathom.

Alexander shifted and took one nipple into his mouth while his hand slid down across her fluttering belly and on toward the source of her excitement. He grazed his hand across her slick heat and then drove his fingers inside her, curling them as he moved them in and out.

Marion was nearly wild with need. She tugged on his shoulders, wanting more and not knowing when and how this would resolve.

"Alexander, please," she whispered.

"Tell me what you want," he said.

"I want you, all of you."

As he drew his fingers in and out of her, he placed his thumb on the most pulsing part of her and within seconds stars burst behind her eyes and a flood of the most delicious ecstasy washed through her veins. Her body bucked and trembled as the sensation continued for what felt like an age. When she opened her eyes, he was staring at her. His fingers were still inside of her and moving in tantalizing circles, coaxing her to continue to squeeze around him.

"Such passion," he said in a voice that was almost a growl. The sound of it touched something deep within her which grew her excitement to build yet again. How that was possible, she did not know, but she was more than willing to find out.

Somehow with him, she found a boldness that was safe to explore. Marion tugged at his doublet and that appeared to be enough for him to remove it and the leine he wore underneath. She marveled at the light hair that dusted the thick muscles of his chest and wondered if his nipples were as sensitive as hers.

She pushed him onto his back and sat atop him, immediately noticing a part of him she'd not realized had changed. She spread her hands over his chest and flicked his nipples with her fingertips.

Alexander grabbed her hips and ground himself against her. "I need to be inside you, Marion."

He flipped her onto her back and tugged her shift off then stood long enough to untie his belt and drop his trews to the floor. She caught sight of him then, tall and lean and fully erect which made her swallow hard. Now she understood what he meant by hurting her. His fingers had not, but this was something entirely different.

Alexander slowly crawled on top of her and shifted her so that her legs were around his back. He kissed her sweetly and a part of her ached as he brushed the tip of his erection against her. She wanted this, wanted everything he had to give her.

"Please, Alexander. I want to feel you inside me."

"Oh God," he whispered and pressed himself against her.

Marion felt a heat that was surprising, and she was glad at first he moved slowly so that she could adjust to him. But as he pushed himself all the way in and then out and back in again, her excitement returned.

She didn't want him to be careful with her any longer. She wanted him unleashed.

HE WAS HANGING on by a thread but was determined to make her first time as easy and pleasurable for her as possible, even if it did mean foregoing his own pleasure. But she kept squirming beneath him, making it more and more difficult to hold on to the control it took to keep from pounding into her which is what he wanted to do.

Marion planted her feet on the bed and thrust upward hard. He took in her state. Head back and grasping at his shoulders, she groaned when he pushed deep within her and held her there, pinned to the bed by his hard cock. She pulsed, and he knew she would soon find her pleasure once again and that was all he needed.

Hooking his arms under her knees, he lifted his hips then thrust hard into her again and again. She was wild beneath him as he neared his own climax but waited until he was sure she had fulfilled her own. On and on he went, thrilled that her body was able to respond to his intense passion with a vigor of her own.

Only when he was sure her quivering had ceased would he allow himself to succumb to his need. He felt the familiar tightening as his climax spread through him and his body shook in all the delicious ways he'd known before, but this time elevated him to such a sense of euphoria he didn't know was possible. He had never felt so powerful and vulnerable at the same time, like his very soul had been exposed in that moment for only her to see.

Still inside her, he released her legs and kissed her softly, willing his breathing to return to normal.

He slid out of her and lay by her side, pulling her to him.

"Are you hurt?" he asked as he brushed a lone tear from her cheek.

"Nay. I am not hurt. I am merely wondering if it will be like this for us all the time and how often we can do it."

Alexander could not help but chuckle. "I have never felt like this," he said. "But I think it will always be like this with us. And as for how often," he said as he kissed her again, "that depends on the needs of my wife."

"Oh really? Does that mean I can have you whenever I like?"

"Aye, wife. You can have me whenever you like."

"Can I have you again now?"

He wondered how he'd managed to find such a woman. And to think he'd thought her experienced at one point. Now knowing with absolute certainty she'd not been, he could imagine all the ways they would pleasure one another in the years to come.

Alexander rolled over onto his back. "You can have me again," he said, his cock coming to life again as she sat on him. Her breasts were round and firm. He reached up to flick one nipple and saw the immediate reaction on her face which he could only describe as pure pleasure, seeing her lick her lips and then bite the bottom one.

"By God, you are beautiful," he said.

He loved the way she slid her hands over his chest as she ground her perfect bottom onto him. He reached down and held his cock while she positioned herself to take him. And take him she did. All the way until their bodies met.

With her head tilted back and her hands on his chest, she slowly rocked her body to move him in and out of her. He did not move as she found her rhythm, but watched as she found a certain spot that was particularly good for her. Her breath came in and out in gasps as she rocked harder and faster, and he could see her climax approaching.

He sought and found her hardened bud and pressed hard then rubbed up and down as she rocked. He held her hip to keep himself from spilling into her as the sight of her revealing her passion was more than any mortal man could bear. She met his gaze as she pushed hard against his cock and his fingers, looking almost wild as her orgasm rode closer and closer.

"Show me your passion, Marion. Show me everything," he said.

She gasped as her body tightened around him so hard, he could hold on no longer. With both hands on her hips, he thrust up into her hard and fast, his own orgasm rushing through his veins at breakneck speed. He threw back his head as a guttural groan erupted from him. By God, he would not survive this, but if he was to leave this world, he could think of no other way he would prefer to do so.

His body pulsed and shook for long minutes as his heartbeat returned to normal. She lifted herself off him and lay by his side. Clearly, she'd found more pleasure in that position, but he could not wait to find other ways to explore the extent of her passion.

And with that thought he was suddenly starving. He pulled a sheet over them both and then sat up to scan the chamber. Their hosts had thought of everything. On a side table was some bread and cheese and meat and a tankard with two goblets.

"Are you hungry?" he asked her.

"Nay, Alexander, I am not," she said, her voice holding a tone of sleepy satedness.

"Do you mind if I sit up for a moment and have something?"

"I don't mind at all," she said, this time even quieter.

Alexander pulled a quilt over her and got out of bed to fill his now rumbling belly. He sat by the small fire for a while, eating a few bites and sipping the mead that had been provided. From time to time, he glanced over at the small mound in the bed. He'd never dreamed such a woman could exist. He'd known some women in his life and had enjoyed those who knew their way around a man's body. But he'd never experienced anything the likes of what they had just shared. She was so unbridled in her expression of passion. He'd suspected they would be compatible from their other encounters, but nothing could have prepared him for this.

Alexander finished his meal and mead and crawled into bed beside her. She was on her side facing away from him, so he wrapped his arm around her waist and pulled her close to his body. He reacted as soon as her firm round bottom touched his cock. It was like she was crafted to perfectly fill his every passionate need.

In her sleep, she pushed back against him when he reached up to cup her breast. She groaned when he lightly pinched her nipple. Alexander reached down and slid two fingers inside her and teased until she was wet enough then slid his now rock-hard cock into her, achingly slowly. He wondered at what point she would awaken knowing he would never dare such an act if her body did not respond, or if he thought for one second she would not want this.

Holding onto her hip, he rocked in and out until he felt her pulse around him. She gasped as her orgasm took hold.

"Oh God, harder, please," she said.

He pulled her up onto her hands and knees and thrust hard and fast and deep within her, his fingers digging into her hips. She clutched the sheets in front of her as she pushed back onto him as hard as he was onto her.

"Harder, please, harder," she said in a whimpering plea.

Alexander gripped her hips harder and slammed his cock into her as hard as he had wanted, holding nothing back as he watched her perfect ass move in front of him and her head tilt upward as she repeated, "oh God" and "oh aye" over and over until she stiffened, and her body tightened around him drawing his seed into her.

She rested on her arms with her head down as her heavy breathing slowed while she still pulsed and twitched. When they were both fully finished, they collapsed onto the bed and Alexander managed to pull the sheets onto them before falling into a deep slumber that offered no dreams or torments, but pure exhausted deep sleep.

CHAPTER TWENTY

MARION JOLTED AWAKE as the carriage dipped and rocked on the road. It took her a few moments to remember where she was and why her body felt like she'd been run over by a dozen horses. She smiled as she recalled just the one stud who was responsible for the soreness between her legs and the tenderness she felt all over.

If anyone had told her that lovemaking with her newly wedded husband would have been like that, she would never have believed them. Despite her mild discomfort, she could not deny she wanted him again and looked forward to discovering all the new ways he'd promised her they would pleasure one another.

They'd risen early the day before and made their good-byes to their hosts and then to her family. She'd hopefully see them again around Yuletide but would spend the remainder of the fall at Inverary Castle as its new countess. She had no idea what was expected of her since Jean had run the place with such perfection; she had no idea how she could possibly live up to her standards, but she would try. She understood Alexander's wishes to return immediately since the issue relating to Jean was unresolved and he did not want it to hang over their heads any longer, particularly when he'd confessed to her all he wanted to do now was enjoy his new wife.

She wondered what he would say if she sat atop him and

woke him up in the same way as she had on their wedding night. She had been dreaming of him, delicious dreams where he kissed and nibbled every inch of her, and the next thing she knew, he was bringing her to full pleasure again, but this time on her hands and knees, and her climaxes just kept coming. She was thoroughly spent by the time her body had been satisfied that she was asleep before she could say good night to him.

They'd stayed at the same inn as before, spending a quiet night wrapped in one another's arms, loving, then sleeping when they wanted and then loving all over again. Marion had never known such bliss could exist.

Now looking across the carriage at him with his head gently bobbing up and down, she thanked whatever power that was responsible for bringing him to her. She could not imagine living without him, and to think she had convinced herself she did not want or need marriage. It turned out she both wanted and needed him.

Looking out through the window, the landscape changed from rolling meadows to sharp mountains off in the distance. She had already fallen in love with this part of the country and now it would be her home. *Their home.*

She supposed now all her parents' focus would be on Alice. They were surely in for a time keeping her in check. But for all her bravery, Marion did wish a similar match as her own. Alice deserved love and happiness. And so did Jean. So what if the man she loved was not an earl or a laird. Love, it seemed, did not discriminate. Would Alexander see that? Would he interfere and keep them apart, or would he let them court properly?

Her own courtship was more than unconventional and with good reason. She could not imagine the passion explosion of the past two days happening out of wedlock. Maybe that was what bothered Alexander so much about discovering the pair, and thinking back, she could now fully understand why he was so distressed. If she were to discover Alice in such a situation, she was sure she would react in much the same way.

She did want to support Jean, but she did not want to interfere with Alexander's decisions. How could she support both of them without seeming to interfere?

"You look like you have the weight of the world on your shoulders," he said, rousing her from her musings.

Turning to him with a smile, she said, "Nay. Just thinking about us and thinking about Jean."

His expression turned from soft and sleepy to concern as his brows drew together. "I know you mean well—"

She put her hand up. "You need not worry. I will not interfere, in that you can be assured. If you want my thoughts, I will happily provide them, but she is your sister, and I will support whatever you decide as you know what is best for her."

Alexander shook his head. "But that is just it. I have not decided anything for her. I left in such a rush to be with you that I did not get the opportunity to truly discover if it is like us, or if it is Alain taking advantage."

"You know him well. Do you think that is something he would do?"

Frowning, he said, "No, I do not. I suppose I was taken off guard having been so distracted by you, and then when you witnessed it, I became even more confused."

Though she was sure he did not mean it that way, a little part of her felt like he was holding her partly responsible for his reaction. Was that a fair way for either of them to think about it? Probably not, but it did illustrate how important communication was in a relationship.

"Would you like my thoughts?"

"Aye, Marion, I very much would."

"I think you should talk to them both separately and then together. Hear what they have to say and then make a decision that makes sense once you know all the facts."

He reached for her and pulled her across to sit on his lap. "How did I become so fortunate to find you?"

She smiled as she stroked his short beard and kissed his forehead. "I do not know, but you must have pleased God in some way."

Squeezing her thigh, he said, "Oh dear, we are not vain, are we?"

"Not at all. I merely tell the truth," she said in a teasing tone.

"I am fortunate," he said. "In all seriousness, I could not have imagined a more perfect partner for me."

"Nor I, husband," she said as she slid off his lap to sit beside him. "About Jean, I do have a question."

"And what is that?"

"Is she still to keep house or will those duties now fall to me? I am not asking to stir anything. I simply wish to know."

"Do you think I would ever assume you would stir trouble?"

"Nay, I just wanted to say that so you would have no reason to think it."

"Marion, I have overreacted where your intentions are concerned and I do apologize for it again, but that is not my general opinion of you."

"I am glad to hear it. I want only the best for us and for your family."

"I know you do, and I love you for it. They are your family now too."

The way he said those words made her insides turn to mush. Moving into a new home, even under good circumstances, was a little nerve wracking as she had no idea if she could step up to fill Jean's responsibilities.

"Are you worried about your new status?" he asked in a soft tone.

"Not really, but maybe a little. I do not want to undermine Jean in any way as I have come to think of her as a friend in the short time I have known her. Maybe she enjoys running the castle. I would not wish to take that from her."

"When I speak with her about Alain, I will ask her. Is that satisfactory?"

"Aye, Alexander, that is perfect, and I thank you for supporting me."

She could understand that it would be awkward for him and her really if she was to be a countess and the responsibilities for running the castle remained with his sister, but she did not want to arrive and then put the place in upheaval.

"All will be well," he said and squeezed her hand.

She hoped so. They rode the remainder of the way without speaking. Marion was sure Alexander was running through in his mind what he would say to Jean, and she was thinking of what she would say as well. She dearly wanted to remain friends with her new sister and understood these first moments with a new mistress could be delicate.

Before long the carriage stopped, and she drew in a deep breath. Hundreds of butterflies were loosed in her belly as Alexander exited the carriage and then stood by to assist her. She stepped out onto the stone walkway and was immediately embraced by Jean.

To Marion's relief, the woman whispered, "I am so very glad you have returned."

Before she could reply, Jean took her by the hand and led her into the castle with a surprised looking Alexander following in tow.

JEAN PRATTLED ON to Marion about how pleased she was to see her and pretty much ignored Alexander entirely. He was concerned enough as it was on the journey home, he wasn't about to wait another day to speak with her.

"Sister," he said, and when she didn't reply, he said it louder. "Sister, I must speak with you."

Turning to him with a frown, she said, "I was about to show Marion the new hydrangea blooms."

"I must speak with you immediately."

Lifting her chin, she walked in the direction of the library and said, "Very well, brother, but only if Marion stays with me."

"So be it," he said and followed them inside and closed the door.

"Well. What is so important that you must speak with me at this very moment?"

"Marion and I are married."

Her jaw slacked and she stared at him for a moment or two before turning to Marion and embracing her. "You are staying with us? And I may now call you sister?"

"Aye, Lady Jean, we are now sisters," Marion said with a smile fully returning the embrace.

"But that means," she said and turned to Alexander, "she is now Lady Campbell, Countess of Argyll."

"Aye, Jean, that she is and that is why I wanted to speak with you straight away. By right, she is now responsible for the running of the castle."

Jean stepped away from Marion and moved over to look out the window. After a few moments she turned and said, "I will show her everything she needs to know, brother. You need not worry about a thing. We will have a smooth transition. But I confess, I will miss some of the duties."

"You may keep some of them," Alexander said.

Jean shook her head. "Oh no, you do not understand. For my lady's sake, she must be seen as in full control even if we speak privately about what needs doing. She must be the person giving the orders or the staff will never accept her. As good as our relationship is with them, this is the way it must be."

"You would do that for me?" he asked.

"Nay," she said as her defiant chin lifted once again. "I will do it for her."

Alexander understood Jean was still angry with him, and he intended to fix that, but for now he was satisfied that her anger did not extend to Marion, for that he could not accept.

"Very well. I thank you for that. Now I also need to speak with you about this business with my steward."

"There is no need, brother. Alain has gone."

"Gone where?" he asked, a knot forming in his stomach.

"He said to tell you that you would know where to find him if you are ever ready to speak to him with respect rather than with accusations."

Alexander nearly chuckled, though that would most certainly be taken out of context by Jean, and likely Marion as well. What neither knew was just how close the two men were, and that Alexander was fully prepared to listen to Alain and, if he was genuinely interested in his sister, he would bless their union.

"I do know where to find him and I will do so after I ask you one question."

"And what is that?" she asked as she placed her hands on her hips.

"Do you love him?"

"Aye, I do love him. And he loves me. And if you were not so pig headed, you would have known that already instead of making terrible accusations against a man you have known most of your life."

He deserved all the pent-up anger she flung at him. In that moment, he could recall their laughter when they thought they were alone. A tryst? Nay, theirs was as real as what he felt for Marion.

"And what are your wishes?"

"I want to accept his proposal of marriage which is what you walked in on. We were on our way to speak with you when you interrupted. But you would not hear reason, and now you've driven away the only man I will ever love, and I will never forgive you for it."

"Jean, I am sure he is not gone."

"Nay, then why have I not heard from him?"

"Because I told him not to and he listened. I will go speak to him now and then we three can sit down together and sort this business. Is that acceptable to you?"

She didn't speak at first but rather stared at him. He hoped she was considering his words to find them sincere.

"Aye, Alex, that is acceptable to me."

"Good. I will leave you two to discuss the transition of duties and seek him out now. We will need new furniture added to my chamber and I would like a hot bath drawn for the countess. She has had a hard ride over a long journey and could use the comfort to ease the ache."

The fully intended hidden meanings were not lost on Marion as he had hoped, and he caught a slight pinking of her cheeks. Thankfully, if Jean noticed, she did not let on that his words were anything but straight truth.

Alexander left the library to find his horse and ride to Alain's cottage. He would apologize in any way the man wanted, but first he wanted to hear Jean's words repeated with as much enthusiasm as he'd viewed in her. He was in no doubt whatsoever of her feelings. If Alain's were in that sphere, he would bless them both and give them whatever they wanted for their future happiness.

Alexander knocked on the door and waited. When he did not get a reply after knocking a second time, he lifted the latch and swung the door wide. The stench of sour ale met him as he entered the cottage and found a sleeping Alain on a cot by the stove.

Shaking his shoulder, he called, "Alain. Wake up." He shook a little harder, which finally did the trick, and Alain blinked awake.

"My lord. What are you doing here?" he asked as he sat up.

"I've come to talk to you about Jean. Come outside. It stinks in here."

Alain stood and brushed his hands through his hair as he stepped outside with Alexander. The man looked like he hadn't slept in days despite having just been awakened.

"You look like shit," Alexander said.

"Aye, I feel like it."

"Alain, I have questions for you."

"I'm listening."

"Do you love my sister?"

"Aye. I do love her, and I want to marry her."

"How long have you been secretly meeting with her?"

"Just the once. We have only spoken one time prior to that of our feelings, but we have noticed one another for a long time."

Alexander watched how Alain's face softened when he spoke of her. He was convinced of two things in that moment. What was between Alain and Jean was real, and he was the biggest arse in all of Scotland for not recognizing it earlier.

"Very well. I give you my blessing. We can discuss the details of her dowry after dinner this evening. For God's sake, get a wash and put on something clean," he said with a grin. "You stink as much as your cottage."

Instead of laughing, Alain crouched down and placed his face in his hands. A small sob erupted from him before he wiped his eyes and then stood and reached his hand out.

"Thank you, my lord."

"You will henceforth call me brother, for after you are wed, that is what we shall be."

Alain gave him a watery smile. In truth, he was exactly the sort of man he'd always hoped Jean would find. But none of the young eligible gentlemen displayed half the wit or gallantry as Alain. His heart was light for this result. This would bring about a new turn for all of them.

As he turned to gather his horse's reins, he realized he'd not spoken of Marion. When he turned back to say something, he saw that Alain had been looking skyward with his hands together in prayer and mouthing thank you. Alexander was so moved by the sight he forgot the words he was about to say. He vowed to himself he would make up for whatever torture he'd put him through over the last several days. For he could not imagine what it would have been like had someone made the determination he could not be with Marion when he had made up his own mind. But he did not require the same kind of permission Alain did. Permission came with his current station and with that many privileges. He would be certain to remember that in the future. Alexander mounted his horse and turned to take the short road back to the castle. This evening would be a time for celebration and joy as he would invite the village to come welcome their new countess and announce the betrothal of Alain and Jean. And then another thought occurred to him. He would need to find a new steward.

CHAPTER TWENTY-ONE

THOUGH JEAN HAD been thorough in her description of the responsibilities she would relinquish, Marion was sure it would take quite some time for her to come into her own as the castle's mistress. One thing was for certain—she would be kept quite busy.

Jean had gone to speak with the butcher as a formal announcement would not be made until later that day and by Alexander, but for now, she found herself sitting alone in the library admiring the way the light cast through the long windows.

"I hear you are to be addressed as Lady Campbell from now on," a male voice said from the doorway.

Alexander's younger brother, Thomas, leaned against the door frame eating an apple, his eyes narrowing as he looked her up and down.

"Aye, that is correct." She had to admit, now that she outranked him, she was not certain what to call him.

"You know you are not the first woman who was considered for the position."

Marion had heard that Alexander had been betrothed before, but that was all she knew about the matter, and it was not something that concerned her so she would just as soon not know at this point.

When she didn't answer, he said, "As the new mistress, my

lady, you should be aware of the kind of man that is your husband, who discards women when he is finished with them."

"I am certain I know my husband well enough."

"Do you? Do you really know my brother that well?"

In truth she did not, but she knew him as well as she could have in their short acquaintance and certainly enough to suss out the sort of man he was which was honorable and good.

"What is your point, Thomas?" She did not mean to use a short tone with him, but he was clearly there to stir trouble as she'd been told he was oft found doing.

He sauntered into the library wearing a smirk that made her insides uneasy. There was something about him that she disliked but was unable to fully put her finger on.

"I merely want to tell you about the man you have married. The kind who sullies innocent lasses and then tosses them aside."

"Thomas, I do not know what you are talking about, but I have many things to do so, if you don't mind," she said as she stood, hoping he would understand the signal for dismissal.

"Oh, but I do mind, Lady Campbell. I came here to tell you about his lordship's first betrothal, and I will have my say."

Thomas stood closer to the door than she, but she still felt as though a thick cloud of dirt had just surrounded her. But she would eat her own tongue before she let him know the effect he was having on her. He took a couple more steps toward her, his eyes glinting with mischievousness.

"Your brother will return at any moment. I suggest you have your say with him and not me, for his past affairs are not my concern."

"Are they not? When they illustrate the kind of man you have married? When the telling may spare you future strife?"

By these statements, Marion had married a cold-hearted monster and that was a very different picture than the one she had developed in her own mind—quite the opposite, in fact.

"I appreciate your warning, Thomas. It is duly noted, but I must beg you leave me to my work."

"Very well, Lady Campbell. 'Tis your funeral."

Was that a threat? God's teeth, now her curiosity was piqued but she didn't want to give him the satisfaction of knowing he'd gotten under her skin.

Marion turned back to the window and gazed out onto the garden which was still mostly in full bloom. It would soon fade as fall approached, but she would find time to enjoy as much time outside as she could before the cold north winds took hold. A little bit of that north wind seemed to try to creep into her heart. Damn Thomas for his troublemaking. She didn't want to doubt Alexander, not now and not ever.

But if he'd had a broken betrothal in the past, was it his responsibility to tell her or was it fair that he kept it to himself? Perhaps he was upset by it still and that thought did not give her any additional comfort as seeds of jealousy sprouted in her heart. The thought of him with another woman made her belly twist and coil. Oh God, Thomas had succeeded if he had meant to torment her. She despised feeling this way. She pined for the euphoria she'd felt in the past days with Alexander.

Marion closed her eyes and envisioned his face smiling at her. She pictured his arms around her and his deep voice calling her name.

"Marion, are you unwell?" his voice asked.

She opened her eyes, heat flooding her cheeks at being caught in a state of emotional turmoil.

"I—I do believe I am," she whispered.

His brows drew in tight as he approached her and led her to the seats near the tall shelf filled with manuscripts that had so fascinated her the first time she'd visited.

"Marion, please. You look as though you've seen a ghost."

"I am not unwell, my lord. Thomas has been to see me."

"Thomas? What did he say to you?"

Marion did not want this to turn into a confrontation. She wanted to sort through her overactive mind and reconcile the flood of thoughts his words evoked.

"He spoke of your first betrothal," she said quietly.

Alexander stood and raked his hands through his hair then swiped his hand over his face.

"And I'm certain he was not kind in his telling of the story. I do hope your opinion of me has not changed," he said, staring hard at her.

She opened her mouth, but the words would not come, so she shook her head, hoping he would understand. Her opinion of him in fact had not changed at all, nor her feelings, but his reaction told her there was definitely more to the story.

"Would you like to tell me about her?" she said, fighting hard to keep her voice from shaking. Did he love her then? Did he love her still?

"I told Thomas that I would tell you about her in my own time and in my own way. My brother has a penchant to stir trouble when he is not occupied with a task and that is my folly."

He paced as he spoke of a woman he'd not met, who he felt had emotional difficulties that would not improve upon living in and being responsible for a castle and its successful running. The betrothal had been set up by his father years earlier when Alexander was but a wee lad.

His voice softened when he sat by her and took her hands in his. "Marion, the poor lass was like a frightened lamb. She wailed the entire time she was here, in this library, upon our first meeting. She was terrified and I had to reason with her father to not leave her here. He agreed and the betrothal was dissolved quietly. I thought I was doing her a favor."

This was a much different account of what Thomas said, but she was still convinced there was more to this story.

"And where is she now?"

Alexander leaned forward, resting his arms on his legs with his head in his hands. Marion's heart squeezed at the sight of him. Curse Thomas for putting them through this right now.

"She is dead," he said.

Marion held her breath.

Alexander sat back and held her gaze. "Her father quickly married her to someone else who was not as patient as I attempted to be, nor as kind. The lass took her own life on her wedding night."

"But why does Thomas hold you on account for her?"

None of what he said made sense.

"The thing to remember about Thomas is that he does not like being second oldest, but he also does not like that I work very hard to keep Inverary and our clan healthy and happy. He has latched on to that past tragedy as something I could have prevented and deems it my mistake versus an unfortunate circumstance."

"Alexander, I am so sorry. He was so convincing that you were somehow responsible and that I was somehow in danger."

He tilted her chin up and leaned toward her. "I promise you with every fiber of my being, you are safe with me and always will be."

His eyes sparkled blue from the light coming from the window, emphasizing the intensity of his declaration. She knew that from that moment on, she would never doubt him again.

HE WAS GOING to string Thomas up by his ears and let the ravens have at him when he found him. This was the final straw with him. All the years of stirring trouble here and there, it was finally going to come to a head. He could see in Marion's eyes, that Thomas had gotten her to doubt him, just a little bit with his version of what had happened. But what he hadn't counted on was that theirs was a connection on a level Thomas did not know existed. Like their souls had spoken to one another.

Alexander found Thomas in the stable, eyeing the stable hand assisting a mare with her new foal.

"A word," he said to Thomas who jumped slightly at the sound of his voice.

"I'm sorry, my lord. I'm a bit busy at the moment."

"But not too busy to frighten the new lady of this castle, though, right?"

Thomas glanced at the stable hand then walked past Alexander and outside. Once they were away from prying ears, Alexander said, "What right do you have to speak to my wife in the way that you did?"

Thomas wore a bored expression when he said, "I told you before, someone had to tell her what she is in for."

"And what is that?"

"That you use and discard people, brother."

Alexander raked his hand through his hair. "I will never understand why you put the blame on me for Eileen's death. She was not married to me. I did not lay a hand on her, Thomas."

"She was terrified of you. I heard her crying to her father to not leave her with you, aye. But he then married her to the worst man in Scotland."

Alexander did not want to think of that, of the fate that resulted in the broken betrothal, but he still did not feel the entirety of it should be laid at his doorstep.

"She smiled at me. Did you know that?" Thomas said quietly after a time.

"What do you mean? When?"

"The day after you tossed her out. I was in the village and saw her with her father. She was not wailing then. She seemed shy and quiet, and she smiled at me."

His gaze drifted to somewhere over Alexander's shoulder for a moment, before he masked his expression again. "But then she was married off shortly after so as to save her reputation from being discarded by you, and now she is gone, and no one will ever be able to show her that not all men are beasts."

"Thomas, I am not like her husband. I did what I thought was right and her father agreed. She would have never survived here as the lady of the castle. If you think about that, you know it to be true. I have mourned her. I am sorry that things ended up the way they did for her, but I am not responsible for her death."

For long moments, Thomas stared at Alexander, seeming to search for what? Sincerity? Eventually he shrugged and shook his head.

"I will always hold you partially accountable, but I will concede I did not need to tell your wife in the way that I did. I will apologize to her when I next see her."

"Aye, that you will, and if I hear of you stirring any further trouble, you will leave these lands and will not be permitted to return. In truth, Thomas, you should be finding your own path in the world instead of trying to interfere in that of others."

"Sage words coming from you who have had everything mapped out for him from the start. What am I to do, brother? Tell me, do."

"Thomas, you have lands you can work. Father has left enough for you to build your own castle. Find a wife and settle down. Stop thinking of the past and look to the future."

"I—I don't know how," he said quietly.

"Well, you can start by attending the feast and really paying attention to those gathered. Tonight, we celebrate my nuptials along with the betrothal of your sister."

"Jean is to be married?" he asked with raised brows.

"Aye, she and Alain are betrothed. I have blessed the union and tonight we shall celebrate in the best way we know how with many stories and much music and merrymaking."

"You sound like Father," Thomas said with a half-smile.

In truth, he sort of felt like the man who, despite their differences, was instrumental in creating an enjoyable feast that they still tried to replicate.

As they walked back to the castle together, Thomas said, "Thank you, Alex."

The words caught him off guard. Thomas had not spoken a kind word to him in years.

"For what?"

"For being patient with me and for being honest. I have been angry for a long time and now realize that was misplaced. The truth is I do not feel worthy of our name," he said and looked up, "of this castle. I see you work so hard to make our family and staff and even the villagers happy, and I know I could never do what you do."

Alexander did not know what to make of his confession. It was true, Thomas's gifts had not yet revealed themselves, but for him to transform so wholly and completely before him was at least a good start for him to find a clear path forward that did not include causing trouble.

"I have a job for you, if you will take it."

"What is it?"

"It is not meant to demote your status in this family in any way but rather teach you the ways of running a large estate as its laird."

"You want me to replace Alain, don't you?" he said with a smile.

Thomas had always been quick-witted which was why he had always been able to get under people's skins so effectively. Very little was missed in his inspection.

"Aye, Jean and Alain will be gifted the manor house and those lands, and he will be busy building a life with her. You will need to learn how to be a good landlord and how to responsibly handle staff and coin. You are keen and know how to read people for deception which will come in handy when you are laird of your own keep."

By the time they entered the castle, they had already mapped out the immediate duties Thomas would take on which included collecting rent from the tenants. That act would teach him how to work with those who were not so fortunate in their birthright.

With Thomas sorted for the time being, he next sought out Jean. Finding her in the library with Marion, he was pleased he could put a smile on both of their currently frowning faces.

"Sister, we will have an additional guest at the feast this eve," he said.

"Oh, and who might that be?"

"Your betrothed will be joining us. As will a newly appointed Thomas as my steward."

"What?" Jean asked. "You have spoken with Alain?"

"Aye, I have, and I have given him my blessing which leaves me without a steward. I have also spoken at length with Thomas, who will be apologizing to you, my lady," he said to Marion. "He has already been given duties to start, and I hope that by him learning how to manage this estate, he will soon move off to oversee his own."

Marion moved to his side. "Are you certain of this?" she asked, concern resting in her beautiful eyes.

"Aye, my love. He is genuinely sorry for the angst he has caused you and me, and we both agree, he needs something constructive to occupy his time."

Four arms wrapped around his middle and squeezed.

"Thank you, brother," Jean said.

"Thank you, my love," Marion said.

Alexander stood there with the two women he loved most in the world hugging onto him, and if he didn't have a feast to help prepare for, he would have stood there all day.

Jean was the first to release him. She wiped her wet cheeks and smoothed her hair. "I don't have time to stand around all day," she said. "I must speak with the cook."

She was halfway to the door when she turned. "I am sorry, Lady Campbell. I overstepped."

Alexander looked down to see that Marion had not thought either that, in fact, it was she who would now have to speak with the cook.

Marion released Alexander and went to link arms with Jean. "We shall go together," she said.

After they left, he placed his hands on the desk and leaned on it. Great fortune had befallen him the day he'd met her. He smiled to himself as a vision of her passed before his eyes with her flaming red hair blowing gently in the wind. That sight was now reserved for him and him alone as she was now required to cover it wherever she went. He couldn't wait to show her later just how happy she had made him.

CHAPTER TWENTY-TWO

MARION'S HEART WAS full. The emotional turmoil of earlier had completely passed out of her the moment Alexander had returned looking content and relaxed. She was keenly aware that whatever the encounter with Thomas, it had ended in a manner that pleased him, and that was good enough for her.

Now in their chamber and stepping out of the bath, she scanned the gowns the maids had selected from her chests to choose which she would wear. Spying the crimson brocade one she'd worn the day she first laid eyes on Alexander, she recalled how she had tried to hide her bosom. With a grin, she wrapped herself in a robe and lifted it for better inspection. Oh, her mother had been cheeky indeed. Inside the bodice was a modesty scarf built in which she could have used that day. Was that part of what Alexander had noticed in her? She'd had a sense from him that he wasn't sure of her motivations in the beginning, and she couldn't blame him. Tonight, she would don this gown again and wear it so that all of her features were accentuated.

The maids entered the chamber a short time after to help fix her hair under a wimple and newly crafted gable hood that her mother had initially intended for her to wear that day. It would take some time to get used to it, but tradition was what it was.

Before long, she was fully dressed and ready to attend to her guests as Lady Campbell, Countess of Argyll, and she was pleased that she fully looked the part. A knock at the door was followed by Alexander who had his clothes gathered and brought to one of the other chambers where there was a bath for him.

He was donned head to toe in black which was a color she was fast coming to love, especially on him. The sight of him took her breath away.

"I remember this gown," he said with a growl as he moved to her and placed his hands on her waist. "But I don't remember your breasts looking this delicious. Have you done something to them?" he asked with a devilish gleam in his eye and a sideways smile.

"Nay, my lord. I have merely allowed them to fill the gown as it was originally made."

"You mean you purposefully altered the way it would fit for modesty's sake that day?"

"Aye, I did."

"And I am now very glad of it, for I and others may have made quite the fools of ourselves tripping over one another to speak with you."

"Because of my breasts?" she asked, unable to withhold a light laugh.

"Aye, we are but men, my love. Sometimes, we are not as deep as you would wish us to be."

She knew he was jesting, and he was certainly not like that, but she would concede there were others who were that shallow. In any case, she loved the way his eyes traveled over her body. If he kept that up, they would not make it to the feast at all. She smiled when he kissed the side of her neck.

"My lord, we have guests."

"I don't care about them," he said as he nipped at her tender flesh just below her ear. "I only need a few minutes. Come here," he said and turned her around then bent her over the bed.

Marion felt her skirts being lifted and a cool breeze on her backside as he exposed her fully and stroked her. Her body was ready for him in an instant. She moaned and a shifting of clothes was followed by him thrusting hard inside her. Her fingers gripped the coverlet tightly as his hard, quick rhythm brought her higher and higher to what she knew would be a brilliant explosion.

Imagining the sight that would befall anyone who might enter had her smiling from ear to ear as she enjoyed the way his hands held her hips so tight and even the slapping way his legs hit hers when he drove himself deep within her.

"Oh God," he said, and she felt him thicken and harden even more. The sensation set off her first orgasm, and by the time he was stiff and rocking behind her, she'd hit on her second.

Waves of delicious flickers washed over her as though tiny sparks shot through her veins. He held her for long moments and then slipped out of her and put her clothes back in place. When she stood, she swayed a little and he caught her in his arms and kissed her softly.

"Did you like that?" he asked.

"Aye," she said. "I did not know we could be so quick as that if we wanted to."

"We can do whatever we like," he said. "And look," he said as he drew her toward the mirror. "Not a hair out of place. No one will ever know but us."

Well, her cheeks were flushed, but he was right. Her gown showed not a wrinkle, and her hair wasn't out of place, because it had been neatly wrapped up. Nothing could compare to the feeling of his naked body pressing hard against hers, but this quick tumble and in that position was more than agreeable to her and she hoped it would be a regular occurrence.

"You have an evil look in your eye, wife," he said.

"I was just thinking how fortunate I am to have such a virile husband."

"That is because he has a wanton wife who is insatiable."

She gasped and swatted his arm. "I am not wanton."

He wrapped his arms around her and kissed her soundly on the lips. "You are wanton and I would not have you any other way."

Marion cupped his face with her hands and kissed him back with all the love and joy she possessed for him. When she pulled back, she said, "I love you, Alexander Campbell, my black rider."

Tilting his head, he asked, "Your black rider?"

"Aye. I recall the first moment I saw you atop your steed decked out head to foot in black with only your icy blue eyes visible under your helmet. I thought you were the most mesmerizing thing I had ever seen."

"You never told me that," he said and became a little quiet.

"What is it?" she asked.

"I recall when I first saw you as well, my exquisite wife. But I'm embarrassed for what I thought then."

"Tell me, Alexander. We are husband and wife now and we shall have no secrets between us."

"I was struck by you as well," he said. "But I thought your parents and you were like all the others in attendance who were only there to snag a husband and did not care how that happened."

"You were not wrong where my parents were concerned, well, mostly my mother."

"But you were not like all the other ladies. I could see that once we met and have found our way of thinking to be so similar. I fell in love with you over and over these past weeks, but the moment that secured it was when you let wee Gordon play his trick on you."

"Oh!" she said. "But he did get me with that one. I was not pretending."

Alexander tilted his head back as a great sound of laughter erupted from him. "Oh, that's even better. Now I love you even more for it."

"Shall we have more stories from him this eve, do you think?" she asked, hoping that would be so. She could spend every evening from thereon listening to them. "And from wee Archie, too?"

"Aye, I think he will be hard pressed to restrain himself now he knows he has an audience and a fan."

Alexander opened the chamber door and hoisted his elbow toward her. "Shall we greet our guests?"

"Aye, my love. We shall."

They walked together toward the great hall, and as they drew closer, the sound of pleasant music and laughter filled the air. Marion had never been so happy in her life, and she was convinced her husband shared that sentiment. They met Jean and Alain just inside the hall near the hearth with a sheepish looking Thomas standing close by. When he saw her, he walked immediately over to her.

"Lady Campbell," he said. "I owe you the deepest apology for my earlier behavior. I want you to know that I sincerely do not wish to make you feel unwelcome or uneasy. My brother and I have talked, and I understand now how deeply I offended you. Will you please accept my apology?"

What could she say but to accept. Everything about the man was in stark opposition to his earlier behavior leaving her in no doubt of his sincerity.

"Aye, Thomas, I accept your apology and am pleased your brother and you have come to an arrangement that will no doubt aid you both."

"My lady is very perceptive. I believe we may become friends in the future."

"Perhaps," she said and moved on to speak with Jean. She wasn't sure if she'd go that far with him yet, but she could find it in her heart to forgive him for his transgression.

ALEXANDER LOOKED AROUND the table at those he'd asked to be gathered for this evening's feast. Others from the surrounding village would join them later, but for now he only wanted his family. Thomas was unusually quiet, which was a blessing but also meant that he had taken their conversation seriously. Jean and Alain had their heads bent together, talking quietly, and Marion was busy with little Archie who had insisted he sit by her. She fit in perfectly with their family and into their lives. It was as though she was always meant to be there carving out a future for them just as surely as she'd carved out a place in his heart.

The coming days and weeks would see them busy and preparing for harvest and stocking up their stores for the winter. They'd always done well for themselves with their proximity to the loch, but he was keenly aware that others struggled. He would see to it the spare pantries were filled as well so that none of his kin would go hungry.

"You are deep in thought," his wife said beside him, urging him from his musings.

"I am thinking of the future," he said.

She looked around the table and then back to him. "They will all require matches at some point."

"I shall never marry," Archie said. "The village lasses are icky."

"You will not always think so, wee man," Alexander said.

"I am a lass," Marion said. "Do you think I'm icky?"

He blushed crimson and shook his head. It was clear that his little brother did in fact not consider his wife icky and might just probably have a wee crush on her instead.

"All is well, wee lad," Marion said to him. "You do not need to like the lasses. I am sure you will find out who you like in your own time, and don't let anyone tell you otherwise."

His little face lit up as she spoke to him, which warmed Alexander's heart. The little ones needed a mother figure in their lives, and while Jean had done the best she could, she needed a little mothering herself. He was grateful Marion would be around to help her prepare for her own wedding which she had indicated she wanted to have during Yuletide as it was her favorite time of the year. Alexander had gladly approved and would have done anything else she asked, so pleased was he that she did not hold any anger toward him from his mistake.

Once the meal ended, they all sat around the large hearth watching little Archie put on a show of telling stories. This, right there, was the only blessing Alexander needed to be fulfilled. They didn't need any of the extravagance they'd experienced at Linlithgow Palace, and he would be forever grateful that Marion did not expect it or crave it, for it appeared she was as contented as he in spending their time with family in such a modest manner.

"Thank you, again, brother," Alain said from beside him. "I believe you have made me happier than I could have ever imagined."

"It is nothing short of what you deserve, my friend. I have always felt you to have the semblance of gentry, despite your heritage."

"I would have your father to thank for that; you know it to be true."

"Aye, he saw in you the man you would become, and I am proud to add you to the family. And before long, you will be adding to it even more!" Alexander slapped Alain on the back and grinned. He'd missed the general teasing that had always passed between them. Alain usually did the teasing. Well, now it was Alexander's turn to return the favor.

Alain gulped and offered a wide-eyed glance at his future wife. "How many children do you think she will want?" he asked.

"That will be up to the both of you to determine," he said in a softer tone, realizing that Alain did not know of such expectations in a family such as this. "You and Jean will have more than a comfortable living no matter how many bairns she wants."

Alain nodded and clasped his hands together. "You have changed my life."

"Nay, Alain. You have changed your life. You did not have to accept all the support my father offered. But you did, and you have used it to become an honorable man who is more than worthy of marrying my sister. And I for one am so very glad you had a wash."

"It was pretty bad."

"Aye, my horse would not even go near the place," Alexander said, trying to lighten the moment.

"I've asked one of the ladies from the village to come and clean it for me."

"You can do that, aye, but henceforth, I would see you taking up rooms here at the castle. Far away from my sister until you are wed, mind you, but here where you belong."

"You want me to live here?"

"Aye."

"Thank you, Alexander. Thank you."

Alain left then to go speak with Jean again who, after a few moments, promptly jumped into his arms and then beamed a bright smile Alexander's way.

He'd done it. He'd fixed his mistake. He'd married the woman of his dreams, and his family were safe and happy. What more could a man possibly hope for?

"You look rather pleased with yourself," Marion said beside him, taking his hand in hers.

"Aye, I am very pleased with myself, wife. I have everything to be grateful for, including the most glorious woman in all of Scotland."

"Just Scotland?" she asked in a teasing tone, prompting his gaze to dip to her neckline then back up to meet hers again. He couldn't believe that just a few weeks ago she'd been mortified to wear a garment that offered such a view, but he loved the way she now embraced her confidence.

"In all the lands anywhere," he said.

"That's better," she said with a smile that would forever melt him.

"Can I ask you something?"

"Of course."

"I know everything happened with us so quickly we've hardly had time to catch our breath, but do you have any regrets?"

"Nay, Alexander, none. I am surprised how wrong I was,

though."

"About what?"

"Marriage. Wanting and needing a husband. Not knowing how that relationship would bloom into a partnership. I had convinced myself I would be fine on my own as a spinster."

"You would never have been a spinster. But I agree that I had myself convinced that it was my lot to raise my brothers and sisters and look after the castle and the clan. I figured by the time they were all married off, I'd be too old and fat to marry anyone."

Marion laughed at his comment. "Even old and fat, you would be attractive to me," she said. "All this hair could fall out and I wouldn't care," she said as she ran her fingers through his hair.

"And bald too, you'll be the death of me, woman."

"I certainly hope not."

"And what do you think of marriage now?"

"Every day I get to wake up to a man who excites and fulfills my every want and need. I had no idea this could be possible, or I would not have delayed my coming out."

"You delayed your coming out?"

"I did and I was convinced I would be forced to marry some old, bald, fat man."

"Stop your teasing, lass, or I will have to punish you."

"Oh! And what do you have in mind?" she asked.

His body reacted immediately to her teasing. All she had to do was lower her tone just a little, sounding husky, and his body was practically ready to take her again.

"You'll see if you keep that up, and we have hours yet before we can retire."

"Oh, there must be a quiet, dark corner around this old castle somewhere."

"Do you want to find out?'

"Aye, my husband. I believe you have a study, do you not? Maybe we need to review some of the accounts that cannot wait."

"I believe you might be right," he said and took her hand, practically dragging her to the study. If anyone noticed, they said nothing, and in truth, they were not gone long enough for anyone to raise any alarm, but what was raised was swiftly satisfied and the sentiment returned. Alexander thought about all the nooks and crannies a large castle like this one would have. And he would explore each and every one of them with her for the rest of their lives.

EPILOGUE

MARION ROLLED OVER onto her back and rubbed her swelling belly. She'd finally gotten her bump within the last fortnight, and she couldn't keep her hands from touching it. And if she wasn't touching it, Alexander was. He'd even placed his ear to it and talked to the growing bairn within her, for he was convinced 'twas a wee lad and was already choosing names.

She lay there for a few more moments enjoying the quiet of the early morn and the fact that the sickness that had plagued her for the first few weeks had fully passed now. She smiled as she got out of bed and donned her robe to sit by the fire. Today Jean and Alain would wed, and the excitement throughout the castle and the village was enormous.

Thick garlands with strings of bright red berries were strung all over the great hall and their small chapel. The aroma coming from the kitchens for the past few days was enough to make a person drool in ecstasy with each delectable dish. Marion had seen to every detail. Her transition to head of the household was not as daunting as she'd thought, and the staff were considerably kind and patient with her when she ordered the wrong things together for dinner or not enough supplies for a particular meal.

But she'd weathered it, and Jean and she had become as close as sisters could be. Unlike her preparation, or lack thereof, she had offered much advice and detail about what would happen on the wedding night. While the conversations were sometimes uncomfortable, Marion made sure Jean knew what to expect.

Marion opened her chest for her new gowns. Alexander had ten new ones made so that they could expand with her and while she was only just showing, she was excited to wear one of them today. She selected a deep forest-green brocade gown with her favorite gold stitching on the sleeves and neckline and laid it on the bed. Alexander had risen early to spend the morning with Alain and to help him be ready for the day.

It was so exciting having a wedding to look forward to before the long cold days of winter set in. She was thankful that she would at least have the bairn growing in her belly to distract her through those awful months. Jean and Alain would remain at Inverary as well until the spring when they could move formally to the manor house, though Alexander and Alain had made regular trips to set it up properly with furnishings and determine sufficient staff.

When she was fully dressed, she left her chamber to see to Jean. The sight that met her upon entering Jean's chamber was breathtaking. Jean wore a deep-crimson brocade gown with a yellow gold wreath on her head, accentuating her beautiful features.

"My dear, you are stunning," Marion said to her.

Jean turned to her with watery eyes. "I never thought this day would ever arrive."

From behind them, Alexander cleared his throat. "Are you ready?" His voice was quiet and gentle. He'd grown closer to his siblings in the past months if that was even possible. And Marion loved him more with each passing day.

"Aye, I am as ready as I can be."

Alexander walked with Jean, and Marion followed to the chapel which was lit with hundreds of candles that were reflected in the berries on the garland. It was warm and welcoming as they took their places. Marion reflected on her own as the priest spoke of the blessing of marriage at this holy special time. Though Jean had specifically wanted the wedding to take place on Yule, the priest was not about to let them forget the Christian significance as well.

Once the ceremony was over and they'd returned to the great hall, the feasting began. Hundreds of people moved in and out of the hall throughout the day and evening as clansmen and villagers flocked to see the common man who'd married into such an important family. For Marion, the thing that pleased her the most was that the family in question did not put on any airs that they were any different than anyone else and she supposed that was why they were so beloved in the region.

At the end of the evening and upon retiring, she sat by the fire in her robe with her husband combing her hair. He'd gotten into the habit of it during her early pregnancy as it became soothing to her. Now he did it because he told her it relaxed him as well.

It had been many weeks since they'd last been together in that way, and many evenings he complied with her wishes to sleep elsewhere as she did not want him listening to her losing her guts all night long. It was certainly not the image she wanted him to have of her in their bed.

"How do you feel?" he asked like he did every evening.

"I feel wonderful," she said. "But maybe a little hungry."

He stopped brushing. "Did you not have enough to eat at the feast?"

"Aye, I had plenty of food."

"Then what do you want? I will get it for you."

She turned to him and let her robe slip open enough to expose her swollen breasts.

"Marion," he whispered. "We can't. You are ill."

"I am ill no longer and 'tis perfectly safe."

"You are sure? How do you know 'tis safe?"

"I have spoken with the midwife, and she assures me not only is it safe, but is encouraged because it helps the mother relax and a stress-free mama is a healthy one."

Alexander appeared to need no more encouragement. With

great care, he lifted her from the chair and brought her to the bed. He gently laid her upon it and then removed his clothes and joined her under the covers.

He stroked her arm and brushed his fingers across her breasts and nipples, sending thrilling shivers through her.

"Are you cold? I will get another cover."

She laughed lightly. "I am not cold, Alex. I am hungry for my husband to pleasure me, and I am not so delicate that I will break."

"You are sure?" he said again.

"Aye, stop asking me that. I am sure. Now do as you are told and take away this ache that you put in me every time you are near me.

Alexander slid his hand into her hair and drew her close for a soul-stirring kiss that she felt right down to her toes. The reverence in that kiss was such that she would never forget for the rest of her days. This was not the hungry insatiable passion they'd initially shared, rather a slow and steady never-wavering passion that would see them through the coming years. Her soul sighed as he rolled onto his back, clearly still thinking she was so fragile. Well, she would give him this for tonight, but after this she would show him that they could love each other as often and however they liked.

She crawled on top of him and slid onto his hard erection. God, she'd missed this so much. The way his eyes grew darker when the passion was in him, the way he gripped her hips, gentler than normal, but holding on nonetheless like his life depended on it.

Marion rode him as hard as he would let her, stilling her if she got too excited. But she didn't want to slow down. She wanted him to lose himself as he had so many times before and for this to pleasure him as much as her.

Reaching down, she spread her hands across his chest and flicked his nipples with her nails. Then she pinched one and loved that way his cock pulsed inside her. Feeling brave, she pinched them both at the same time and squeezed her womanhood around him. Air hissed through his teeth as he turned their bodies and pulled out of her so that she was on her belly. He lifted her hips and thrust hard inside her once, twice, and reached around to rub her clit. Her orgasm hit her hard and fast as he stiffened behind her.

"Christ," he said as he slid out of her and lay by her side to stroke her hips and arms and breasts. "You don't have to grin like you've just won a great prize," he said with a chuckle.

"But I have won a great prize. I do not think you are so opposed to me winning that prize, are you, my love?"

"I would never deny you anything in this world, even if it means letting you seduce me."

"I should hope you want me as much as I want you," she said, already knowing the answer. They lay like that for a while, staring into one another's eyes, touching each other softly.

He rolled on top of her and spread her legs wide. "You are sure it is safe in all the ways we love one another?"

"Aye, that is what I have been told."

"Then this is how I want to have you."

He kissed her slowly, his tongue dancing with hers as he entered her all the while staring into her eyes. "I want to watch you reach your peak," he said as he hooked her legs up over his back.

His movement increased as he brought her higher and higher toward that final release she achieved each and every time they joined.

"Marion, my love, my life," he whispered as he brought her to her climax and reached down to pinch her clit to hold the ecstasy. She exploded over and over again thinking she could take no more, and when the one ended, another began. For what seemed like an age, he watched her as her body shivered and shook in pure delight. When it was over and she was completely spent, he wrapped his arms around her and pulled her tightly to him.

Her heartbeat took a while to slow as she lay there in his arms and thanked the pagan gods, and hers too, for making and bringing her a man like him. Her life and the life they were building together was more than she could have ever hoped for.

"I thought of another name for our wee laddie," he said.

"And how can you be sure 'tis a wee laddie?"

"Oh, I just know when he speaks to me. He tells me he can see how beautiful his mammy is on the inside so she must be very beautiful on the outside and he can't wait to meet you."

Marion choked back a sob. That was the most beautiful thought she'd ever heard, and though 'twas impossible, she would hear him express such thoughts for all time.

"How did I get to be so fortunate to find you?"

"I don't know, love, but I'm very glad you did. And I'm glad for whatever force it was that brought me to you, even if it did cost me a concussion."

Marion lifted her head. "What?"

"I said nothing."

"You fell because you were thinking of me?"

"Go to sleep. You're hearing things."

"I will ask Alain. He'll tell me."

"Alain will tell you nothing," he said and kissed her on the forehead. "Now go to sleep, you and the bairn."

She snuggled down wearing the biggest grin of her life. She'd get him to admit it one day. And before long, she did exactly as she had been told; she fell asleep feeling safer and happier than she ever had in her life, knowing that when she woke, he would still be there with her and for all the days and all the bairns to come.

THE END

About the Author

Amazon internationally bestselling author of the award-winning Highland Chiefs series, Kate Robbins writes historical romance out of pure escapism and a love for all things Scottish. She thoroughly enjoys the research process and delving into secondary sources in order to blend authentic historical fact into her stories. Ranging over a thousand years, Kate's novels are filled with passion, adventure, and political intrigue. Kate is the pen name of Debbie Robbins who lives in St. John's, Newfoundland and Labrador, Canada.

Facebook:
facebook.com/KateRobbinsA

X:
x.com/KateRobWriter

Instagram:
instagram.com/robbins.kate

BookBub:
bookbub.com/authors/kate-robbins

Amazon:
amazon.com/Kate-Robbins/e/B00FRHRUPE

YouTube:
youtube.com/channel/UCpmDa4KgxFVKqoTK0CS6SRg

Goodreads:
goodreads.com/author/show/7328484.Kate_Robbins

TikTok:
tiktok.com/@robbins.kate

www.ingramcontent.com/pod-product-compliance
Lightning Source LLC
Chambersburg PA
CBHW060402310726
48976CB00003B/915